THE HOLLYWOOD GRAIL

BOOKS BY GORDON STRONG

NON-FICTION

Stanton Drew and its Ancient Stone Circles
King Arthur, the Waste Land and the New Age
Sun God and Moon Maiden: The Secret World of the Holy Grail
Brides Mound: Gateway to Avalon
The Sacred Stone Circles of Stanton Drew
The Way of Magic
Merlin Master of Magic
Tarot Unveiled
The Five Tarots
The Qabalah: Beyond the Veil
Lion of Life: The Spiritual Life of Madame Blavatsky
The Golden Dawn: A Key to Ritual Magic
The Magical Character

FICTION

Dawn of the Goddess
Sir Norbert and the Purple Haze
Doorway into Darkness
Windleroot
The Empire of Evil

The American Trilogy:
America Dreams
Windows of Heaven
Only True Love

THE
HOLLYWOOD
GRAIL

GORDON STRONG

Cover design by Jonny Clooney

First Edition 2015

ISBN 978-1-909356-12-2

DIOSCURI PRESS

Published by Dioscuri Press
Dublin, Ireland

www.dioscuripress.com
enquiries@dioscuripress.com

CONTENTS

Thunder is good, thunder is impressive; but it is lightning that does the work.

— **Mark Twain**

… the greatest loves of our lives exist out of this world either in the long past or the unrealised future.

— **Arthur Guirdham**

All you need to make a movie is a girl and a gun.

— **Jean Luc Godard**

PREFACE

The world of movies defies all logic. Things occur for no apparent reason, and what we assume will happen never does. What was once classic is now cliché.

For Jack Strange, his dream was real—one he believed would come true. Many film directors have thought the same, few have succeeded.

Gordon Strong
Portishead, UK
November 2014

1

"A caller is requesting call-collect from Los Angeles, will you accept the call?"

"Okay."

"That script of yers is the greatest I ever read … I love it."

How could anyone believe a person who said things like that? I certainly didn't. No one ever listened to Avery Biebermann anyway. They probably never did, even from the moment he learned to talk. An executive producer in Hollywood, he talked big but stayed small time. For those who aren't *au fait* with these things, an EP is the guy who gets the money together so a movie can be made. Like every role in the film business, there are countless thousands of people who do the same thing as Biebermann. Some do it better, some a lot worse.

"What's yer budget on this?"

"Ten million."

"That's crazy."

"Is it?"

"Sure, we're talking fifty here …"

"We are?"

"Yeh, let's get … involved …"

Here old hot-shot Biebermann named a galaxy

of stars—one or two I'd actually heard of—before bouncing into the next round of bullcrap.

"Yers is a historical picture, right?"

"Mmm …"

"An' you got the State Film Board involved …"

"They've been very helpful …"

Biebermann sounded like he'd just got a merit mark.

"Not got you funding though did they, huh?"

"No …"

"They tell yuh about *tax incentives*?"

"We didn't discuss that …"

"Listen, you gotta get these things straight before you agree to film anywhere. If we wanna make a whole series of historical pictures … which we should do … then they oughta be helpin' us out."

I suddenly felt incredibly exhausted.

"Maybe."

"You tell anyone over there who wants to invest in yer picture that they can contact me … Avery Biebermann. I'll put up fifty-per-cent."

"Okay, I'll pass that on."

"Yeah, you do that, an' tell 'em to call me."

I clicked off the phone, or Biebermann did. This all took place six months ago, a long time in the movie business. A lot of things had happened since then, and a lot of things happened before that. Let's start at the beginning. This is my movie, my story.

In the 1950s, England looked permanently grey—about as inspiring as a wheelie-bin. To me it was also totally alien, prompting only a great need to escape.

Where would I go? Into the imagination, the land where anything might happen and a lot more does.

Jimmy Edwards, Sir Anthony Eden, Sabrina, Wilfred Pickles. Who were these people? They made no sense to me then, and neither do they now. Authority, society, and the Empire bemused and baffled us when we encountered them at school. Was it all because of the war? We were shown *The Dambusters* and *Reach for the Sky* as if someone was trying to prove a point.

The Goon Show was a valiant attempt at putting the world another way up, rock'n'roll too—the Elvis and Buddy Holly version. Tommy Steele and Cliff Richard just didn't cut it. Neither did Ian Carmichael and Richard Attenborough who, compared to Dean or Brando, had all the charisma of a rollmop herring. You would have had to say that America owned the monopoly on fun—there was no contest.

The programmes on TV looked like they were made in a fog, and scripted by a bank manager. Comics—regarded as trash by the Establishment— were where the magic was. What did all this do to me? Right from the start, I wanted to create a world that I believed in, that others would too. It did not take me long to realise that making movies was about that. Right now, in the glorious present, I regarded my bank statement as a prisoner his death warrant. It did not make for happy reading. Just before I reached for the whiskey and a loaded revolver, my phone buzzed.

"Hey, how y'doin'?"

"I'm okay. I wanted to know what was happening …"

Linda, my girlfriend, did this all the time. She

expected me to know what she was talking about without giving me any clues.

"Us going out?"

"What else?"

My telepathic powers went on hold.

"I thought we decided on that new Greek place …"

Wrong.

"No, I said I didn't want to go there …"

"Okay …"

"Don't you remember I said I wanted to go to *The Golden Wong*?"

"In town?"

There was one of those pauses I had lately come to dread.

"What's the matter with that?"

"Nothing …"

"It just sounded like you didn't want to go …"

"No … I … just …"

The temperature went sub-arctic.

"Forget it then."

"What?"

"We won't go out …"

Before I had time to say anything else the phone clicked off. Our relationship had been like this for some time. I was often amazed that Linda stayed with me. or me with her—just habit I suppose. My mind wandered off in another direction, one that featured fame and untold wealth in ever increasing amounts.

Dave Whitefield could have walked around with a sign around his neck saying 'I'm dodgy', this being evident to anyone with half a brain who encountered him. He always wore the same suit, creases like a razor, his way of doing business being the same. He had texted me several times wanting to meet for dinner, something I couldn't get enthusiastic about. A twinge of guilt made me answer his call.

"Hello, Jack."

Dave's enthusiasm always came over as predatory, fangs exposed for all to see. I was on my guard, the welcome mode set on low to medium.

"How's things?"

"Okay, okay. You're still coming in with me on this project aren't you?"

No recall—exorcised from the memory banks.

"Remind me what I'm supposed to be doing again …"

I heard Dave sighing, prior to the hard sell.

"Really easy. Nothing to it, mate. Just directing your bit … maybe help some of the younger guys with their stuff. Post-production might need five minutes of your time."

"Ah, right."

"So, you up for it?"

I popped in a pause.

"Wasn't there some problem … ?"

Dave reacted as if the word was totally unfamiliar to him.

"No. Don't think so …"

"Being paid …"

Had I said something obscene?

"I can't remember any trouble about that …"

I could, and let him have the details. Silence ensued.

"You still there?"

"Yeah, yeah, I was just thinking. Well, if you'd rather let it go, mate …"

"I would."

"No worries … catch you later."

Talking to characters like Dave Whitefield was a regular part of the day in the movie biz. After all these years, it was still too often for my liking.

The only thing that means diddly-squat in the film world is money. Forget art, vision, integrity—any of those other nice words. It's a business, one that's mindless and greedy. Once the cheque is in the production company's account, they can do anything they want, even blow the whole thing. Over the years, plenty of people have done just that. The secret is that there are no secrets. No one, not even Mr. Smarty-Pants in LA, ever knows why a movie becomes successful.

You could suggest that it's close attention to detail, chemistry in the casting, a great script, or a dozen other factors. You would be wrong on all counts. Although any of these *might* make a contribution, what makes a sure-fire hit is anybody's guess. Nobody will admit that though. Hollywood, because it's Hollywood, thinks it has all the answers. Zillions of dollars have been wasted making crap films. Why? Because some bunch of suits thought they had the magic formula— one that would win them a whole bag full of Oscars. All they were left with was a big, fat turkey, one you couldn't even eat.

When we did eventually go out, Linda decided it *was* the Greek restaurant she wanted to eat at. Thus we found ourselves in *Rousso's*, chomping on kebabs to the sound of balalaikas. In between gazing at the plastic grapes on the ceiling, a feature of the place which had always fascinated me, I regarded my companion. Blonde, with a wide mouth and a better than average figure. I decided, as I always did, that I liked Linda, but with *reservations*. As we didn't live together there were always routine questions waiting to be asked about each other's doings. Hers were always centred on work and the burdens constantly crushing her tender spirit.

"We've got so much on at the moment … it's amazing I could even get out tonight."

"I'm glad you did."

"I've been taking work home every night this week."

Although we had known each other for some time, it was never clear to me what Linda did in her brightly-lit office. The company was something to do with making sails for yachts, at least that's what I had always believed.

"That must be a bit of a bore."

She looked at me in some amazement, more than my remark warranted, I thought.

"Well, what else do you expect me to do?"

"I don't know."

I received a medium intensity glare. Linda had appeared in my life after Christine and I had parted. After being with someone who, with almost surgical precision shredded my emotions, I had been drawn to a woman who was a little more staid. Nature striving for balance I suppose. Both Linda and the previous model certainly shared a tendency to be difficult though.

"How's your latest little thing going?"

She could have been a junior school teacher addressing a difficult child in the class.

"Just waiting for the green light as always."

"That's what all you people always say isn't it? It sounds so silly ..."

"A lot of things sound pretty ridiculous in the ..."

Ulysses, the owner, arrived with more wine at that moment, temporarily saving the day. Linda had lost the thread already and leapt into conversational pastures new.

"When are we going on holiday?"

"In a couple of months?"

"That's no good."

"No?"

"You know perfectly well I'll be working then."

"I thought you had time off in September ..."

"It's been changed."

I tried to remain neutral.

"I'm *sure* I told you ... you probably weren't listening."

I hesitated to defend myself. I was only too aware of the next stage of this game.

"So, when are ..."

"It'll have to be in the next three weeks."

"But ..."

Linda threw down her napkin.

"I know what you're going to say, you're too busy to go ..."

"Well *I am* waiting for ..."

She looked away, pretending to study the mural of the Parthenon.

"I'll go with someone else …"

I poured more wine, with the utmost control.

"If you listen a minute …"

Linda interrupted.

"Don't you want to know who I'll be going with?"

I did not hesitate.

"That bloke who fancies you at your work."

That rather took the wind out of her sails.

"If he asks me I will."

I sipped my wine.

"So, he hasn't yet?"

Reason never conquers anger.

"You don't care do you?"

"Yes, but it sounds like I haven't got much say in any of this."

Linda swallowed some wine and almost choked.

"Oh, you're so ridiculous."

Having ascended to this peak of hysteria, conversation rather subsided. I paid the bill and we left, Ulysses showering us in farewells as we went out the door. Twenty minutes later, while we were walking to my house in Clinton, disaster struck. Linda suddenly announced she did not feel well. She became hysterical and I wondered if she might be sick on the pavement.

Fortunately, a taxi was passing at that moment and I hailed it. Linda seemed to recover, but insisted on going home alone. I gave the driver her address and watched the cab drive away, any prospect of passion disappearing with it.

Everyone believes they know everything about the Sixties—that extraordinary time when everybody wore flowers in their hair, smoked dope, and had endless sex. Some may have done, I'm certain many people didn't. For them, it was the same old world with a touch of psychedelic colour creeping in at the edges. Being on the dole in a council house in Neasden with four kids wouldn't make anyone feel fab, groovy, or anything else.

The first time I ever got behind a movie camera was in 1965. As the singer in a band that had played a few local gigs, it was my idea to film us. I must have been inspired by seeing *A Hard Day's Night* at *The Odeon*. Our drummer's Dad had a Kodak M22 camera with a pistol grip and he generously agreed to lend it to me. We bought four Super 8 cassettes, each of us paying for one. Did the bass player plead poverty and the rest of us subsidise him? Probably— he was like that.

I was smart enough to realise that if everything was shot hand-held the result would be painful to watch. By constructing a tripod, using a drill rig I'd borrowed from the local garage, we got some steady footage. Letting anyone else point the camera was a mistake too, as they would inevitably wave it around like a hose pipe. I shot twelve minutes of film; it was a struggle to get two minutes of usable material out of it, but I succeeded. I made up some boards with the credits—prominently featuring myself as director, cinematographer and editor—and shot those as well.

My first attempt at editing, involving a razor blade and film cement, was a laborious business to say the least. Later I found out about splicing tape and bought a little machine which correctly lined up the sprocket holes. With the benefits of such superior technology, the film jumped about less in the projector. The most valuable lesson I learned from my editing venture was timing the cuts to the sound, pretty sophisticated stuff for a seventeen-year-old.

We had made a live recording of our best song, so I used this as the sound track. Super 8 didn't have audio so we synched up a reel-to-reel tape recorder and showed the film in the Village Hall. It attracted an impressive audience and, flushed with success, I screened it for the whole of the Sixth Form at school. I must have been confident about my talents as a film maker. My next experience a few years later, involving a crew, was a different ball game altogether.

My parents would never have entertained the idea of me going to the B. F. I. School in London so I didn't even bother to ask them. Barstowe was the nearest city to where we lived, the university offering a joint degree in English and Drama. The course, which included acting and theatre production, was close enough to what I wanted. I enjoyed my time as a student, and attained what was generally regarded as a perfectly useless degree.

In my final year it occurred to me that if I made a documentary about our august seat of learning, the university authorities might agree to fund the project. I submitted a shooting script, labouring long and hard over the tone of the piece, a factor much more important than the content. The previous year—1968—had been riven with revolution, Barstowe University not escaping a taste of anarchy. Thus, I played down any reference to social upheaval and things political, highlighting rag week and college revues as a healthy outlet for high spirits. Support from several tutors helped persuade the bursar to part with a thousand pounds—a more than generous sum in those days.

Final approval having been granted by the Vice-Chancellor, we were up and running. Naturally, I drew upon willing friends for most of the crew, but I was ambitious. Having a professional cameraman and soundman and shooting in 16mm was my aim. I found these in Dennis and Rod, a pair who were enthusiastic about the project, mainly because they liked the idea of being surrounded by dolly birds. They may have even scored once or twice during the shoot but, if they did, they kept their successes to themselves. One significant aspect I had overlooked was the real cost of post-production. This would give me problems later on but, flushed with enthusiasm, I planned the shoot.

The premise was simple, to show the university from top to bottom, from the gardeners toiling in the rose beds to speeches at the Senate. The latter, it was insisted by the authorities, had to be filmed in long shot. The rest alternated between the academic life—earnest tutorials, dedicated young scholars— and having lots of jolly fun. The result was acceptable fare—meat and two veg. , neither too bland nor too exotic.

We had to work with our surroundings, and I quickly realised it wasn't going to be easy to get the classic David Lean look, or even a touch of Truffaut. The university buildings were exclusively Victorian Gothic and, although perfect for an imposing tilt, proved to be too much of a good thing. I didn't want my movie to resemble a travelogue, so I went for top shots, looking down on scenes happening in the campus, or in the streets near the administration buildings.

The colour of the stone work was also vexing as it tended to absorb natural light and turn everything into a dull monotone. High tones had to come from the cast—the students themselves. Fortunately it was a time when colour in clothes was startlingly iridescent. I encouraged as much op-art as possible, even among the staff. A cut to a close-up of a paisley tie during a lecture added a little spice when it was needed.

The state of the art, as always, determined the look of the film. Softer than anything seen now, this was partly because cameras in the Sixties could never offer absolutely sharp focus. Kodak 16mm stock had high contrast and made warm colours hot, and blues very cool. A certain translucency, a result of the reversal process, was always there. The lushness too was a legacy of Technicolor, so prevalent in the previous decade.

By using high speed film for interiors, I rang the changes. Because lighting equipment was then so cumbersome I abandoned heavily lit interviews and dramatised pieces. Seen a few decades later, this almost breathless style—following people down corridors and into rooms—has a much greater immediacy. Film has an authenticity only when it depicts what someone might actually be seeing at any given moment.

Given the budget, it would not have been possible to build dolly tracks, so we improvised as best we could. Installing Dennis on a luggage trolley was one idea and, less successfully, wheeling him about on a pair of sack trucks. I also built a harness for a primitive *steadicam*, but without the benefit of any hydraulics. This Heath Robinson device worked remarkably well when it felt like it and failed miserably at other times. I was not popular with Martin when on one occasion the camera fell onto a concrete floor, luckily without sustaining any damage.

My hidden agenda was to make two films out of the footage we shot; the official film—conservative and correct—and a freaky version. I revealed the plan to Martin and Rod early on and they were enthusiastic. Experimenting with the way we went about filming appealed to them. Having attended the London Film School, their technical knowledge was far superior to mine. On occasions they would veto some outlandish idea, but only if it was impossible practically. The 'day's challenge' became part of the routine.

Shooting from every angle we could—from inside

a car or tying the camera to the front of a motorbike—was *de rigueur*. We even took the camera, suitably protected with polythene, into the university pool. I persuaded a camera shop in Barstowe to let me have a fish-eye lens for a day or two on trial. Our usual repertoire of effects—lens flare, coloured filters and slow motion—was in there, along with jump cuts and stop motion. We also utilised the light shows that were popular at the time at rock gigs. We were sometimes allowed to manipulate the back projection, one of the standard features of these shows.

I encouraged any keen photographers to take as many stills on set as they wanted. We tried boiling their film in the developing tank, a process which produced images that resemble cracked glass. We enlarged the best of them to enormous size in the university darkroom, developing the prints on the floor with a squeegee mop. These we used as a backdrop in scenes, alternating them with screen prints and solarised photographs. Screen printing, a process that could eliminate half tones, and one beloved of poster makers of the era, was perfect for titles. An optical shimmer could also be obtained by using two complementary colours of equal tone.

Rod and Martin had talked about the project to a friend of theirs—Jeff who was an editor. He turned up on the last day of shooting and introduced himself. Kitted out in flying jacket and scarf, he had the air of someone who would be accomplished in whatever he chose to do. Having realised I had made no arrangements for editing the footage, here might be the man to do the job. There was only one problem—

with the cost of developing the film stock, and after I had paid Rod and Dennis, there wasn't much left of the budget. All I could do was offer this to Jeff. I boldly did so and, to my surprise and unfeigned delight, he agreed to edit my movie.

Jeff had set up a permanent editing suite in the garage of his home and, in between revising for my finals, I spent a lot of time there. He was a master of the Moviola, and from him I learned the rudiments of the craft. His greatest gift was the ability to look at any footage and discover something I had not seen in it. The art of editing is manipulating reality—creating a new vision. To demonstrate his skills, Jeff would ask me what I wanted to happen and then go ahead and make it happen. I was truly amazed. Choosing the exact frame in the film to make a cut was absolutely crucial in achieving this end; Jeff had skills I could only marvel at.

From him I learned so much that would be valuable later in my career. Judging exactly where tension should occur—building and releasing the emotions between two actors—is the key to drama. Cutting on a reaction was essential to achieving this, and inevitably I could see where I had missed a shot that I should have planned for. I learned the very basic technique of shooting a scene from different angles so as to give the editor as much material as possible to work with, a procedure which quickly became automatic.

Jeff instilled in me that, for any editor, the story is the most important feature; nothing else. From what we had, and we zealously kept the trims in case any odd few frames could be utilised later, we fulfilled my plan—putting together two movies.

When I presented the finished film to the university bigwigs they immediately pronounced their approval. They were certain they owned a cinematic prospectus, a first at the time, and organised an official viewing at the end of the academic year. The Vice Chancellor gave an address in which he said nice things about me and everyone else who had participated.

My graduation ceremony signified the end of my university career. I wasn't enthusiastic about doing an MA, I wanted to get out in the world and make movies. My enthusiasm had been fired the more by the reception given to *Good Scene*—that was the title I had given to the alternative movie Jeff and I had put together. I had submitted the piece to the San Francisco Film Festival—a daring move in more ways than one as I had mailed the only copy of the film to the West Coast of America.

The 1969 San Francisco Film Festival would be forever remembered as the one when sticky stuff got chucked about by the freaks. The police and the festival attendees were very po-faced about it, as well as being pie-faced. Whether that anarchic moment had any effect on the jury's decision to award *Good Scene* a special prize would be impossible for anyone to speculate. But, on the strength of this accolade I was invited to fly over and schmooze with the celebrities of the San Francisco Film Society. It was a nice idea, but I simply hadn't got the funds to get there. It would be another thirty years before I went to California, the heart of the movie world.

3

I nevitably, my parents began to quiz me about my intentions for the future. During my final year I had been distinctly cagey when discussing anything with them. Now there was nothing for it but to announce that I wanted to go into the movie business. This received the response I had expected and, to avoid any further embarrassment, I departed for the city of Barstowe once more. There I found a ground-floor room in Clinton—rents were still cheap in 1969— and took a night shift in a factory to keep myself. My surroundings were far from spacious, but I made the best of what I had. A pay-phone in the hall proved to be a lifeline to my new world.

I followed up every lead in the biz I could. My approach was always to hint that *I* was the man for the job, and no one need look any further. Producers were always looking to fill empty spaces, and I made sure I had the reputation of someone happy to be part of any crew. My willingness to diversify meant I often got the call over someone else.

I considered moving to London but decided at this stage my career was not compromised by being away from the metropolis. By this time, a lot of work had shifted away from the large studios to the provinces. The big change for me came when I met Douglas, Viscount Hampton. This happened at one of those Saturday night parties in Clinton which, even at the beginning of the Seventies, still managed to retain an exotic air.

Sex was certainly on offer when I was a student but—as a legacy from the previous generation—a certain degree of commitment was expected. A lot of my contemporaries started going steady in their first year, some even getting engaged. I deliberately did not get involved with anyone, no matter how attractive. My ambition was to be a filmmaker and nothing must stand in my way. I later learned that such a degree of self-regard is never far from plain arrogance. Tragically, having seen that quality in others, I didn't recognise it in myself.

The scene in Clinton was still considered the hottest ticket in town. From the time the pubs closed, to sashay from one party to another on into the small hours, was considered most hip. The thump of soul music unerringly guided those seeking a scene and, on this particular night, I joined the throng making their way through the open front door of a mews house. Already the revellers were flowing up and down the stairs and eddying into the garden, even into the street. The usual suspects were there in force. Full beards and beery voices identified the old guard, shoulder-length hair and fey features marking the young pretenders.

I passed the time with a few film people I knew, all the time looking around for something or someone new to inspire me. The girls looked mostly spoken for, and I did not purport to be any great stud in those days. Gravitating towards the refreshments in the basement kitchen, the usual fare—Spanish plonk and dry French bread—I was suddenly aware of a tall, insouciant figure among the throng. He was swaying somewhat as he casually introduced himself.

"Douglas …"

"Jack."

"So what do you do?"

As soon as I mentioned movies, even in a self-depreciating way, my new acquaintance immediately became animated. Unprompted, he began to tell me of his own plans in film. Obviously yearning for a confidant, Douglas seemed grateful that I was prepared to listen to him. Apparently, he was about to produce and direct a documentary.

"There's a rock festival happening in a couple of weeks … out in the country. I want to film the whole weekend."

I tactfully withheld my own opinion that, with the Sixties over, pop music now afforded little relevance to contemporary culture or anything else. Douglas was, however, expounding at some length on the zeitgeist.

"It's really important right now to *record* what's going on … at the moment it happens."

I accepted this solipsism for what it was worth.

"Sounds great."

What happened next could be simply explained—at a certain stage of drunkenness, people often act rashly. Douglas promptly offered me the job of co-producer. He did not enquire as to my experience, just assumed that my appearing in his life at that moment was sufficient recommendation. It was also obvious he assumed I would agree to the proposal. My acceptance being *fait accompli*, I could only go along with the idea. Douglas fumbled about in the pocket of his jacket and gave me a card with his phone number on it. On the back he wrote the date when he proposed to meet the organisers of the festival, and asked me to accompany him.

Being stolidly in trade, my Victorian forebears would have had little to do with the aristocracy, except as very occasional customers. The uptight bourgeoisie regarded the privileged classes with the suspicion, even outright horror. It was assumed they were as much lacking in morals as the lower orders. Perhaps inheriting this attitude to some degree, I was never seduced by the supposed charm of dukes and the rest. For me, history demonstrated only too often that rulers maintain their position through servitude and oppression, nothing else. In Medieval England the barons maintained the upper hand by robbery and murder and, in succeeding centuries, the landed gentry hanged any peasant they found on their property. They may be beautifully spoken, but the titled in society are as ruthless as any Mafioso leader. Douglas, Viscount Hampton, was no exception, as I was later to discover.

In those days, Windleroot was a market town, hardly different from any on the Moors. It had not deteriorated into the New Age Disneyland the place was later to become. That change for the worse was heralded by the very event we were to film. Held in the fields of a farm in the nearby village of Pillstown, it was planned as a joyous weekend of music. A hint of ecological concerns, then in their infancy, pervaded the proceedings. Who was to know at the time that the festival was destined to gain international acclaim and become a billion dollar enterprise?

After Douglas picked me up outside the flat, we set off in his rather battered Riley. There were two others in the car, apparently old school friends. I assumed they were part of the crew, but was mistaken in this as they simply disappeared when we arrived at the farm. Girls in long dresses and cotton tops, escorted by young men in jeans and work shirts, were milling around aimlessly. Transcendental types sporting djellabas, with Indian bells clustered at the throat, were to be found among them.

One figure who could not be ignored was Bailey. This apparition, in multi-coloured coat and voluminous flares, combined the persona of a jester and an exiled sultan. He was also a master of the hippie non-sequitur, as were many we met. When we arrived for our initial meeting with Grainey Buttle, the organiser of the festival, Bailey was there at the farmhouse door. Like some exotic butler, he led Douglas and myself into the room where Grainey was holding court. The latter greeted us warmly, full-on hugging having just come into fashion. A good deal of assumed piety had to be endured as well, before we got down to business.

"This gathering is an Earth Fair, and I really *do* want to make that clear to everyone who's part of the festival in any way at all. Every musician, as well as you film people, should realise we are privileged to be standing on sacred ground. Ego-tripping, rock star vibes would be a real bummer in this holy place … we are all on a pilgrimage to discover the Temple of Windleroot."

There were mutterings of assent from the faithful followers. Douglas, I noted, seemed to be quite equal to this kind of cant.

"Sure, sure I can dig that. My whole scene is to make a genuine … respectful if you like … record of the gathering. We consider it a great privilege to do that, and we'll be totally discreet. No one will even notice we're around when they're … doing their thing … whatever it might be."

This kind of talk seemed to go down well. As co-producer, I did not welcome the prospect of conflict—particularly in the ideology dept. Grainey beamed benignly on Douglas.

"I just know you and all your people are gonna be really cool, man. Anything you need, we're here for you."

"Thanks. Nice one."

Despite their hippy regalia, I was certain Grainey and his gang were middle-class types slumming it among the unwashed. They would naturally assume a respect for Douglas as head-prefect. Consciously or not, they still recognised his rank.

During all this, Bailey had been making strange cackling noises, presumably to show his approval. He had rolled a joint of something lethal which was being passed around. I noticed eyes getting redder and heads sinking among the company. Douglas took a quick hit, but I passed on the offer. The whine of a sitar and a pattering of drums could be heard from beyond the window. Grainey smiled—a low key display of ecstasy—and we filed out of the room. Bailey was still grinning like a clown with rigor-mortis surrounded as he was by a halo of dope smoke.

When I mentioned this oddity to Douglas he just shrugged and said he was 'a bit of a character'. Obviously he regarded Bailey as one who personified the spirit of the times. I was not convinced, certain he should not to be trusted, and deliberately ignored him whenever possible. Later, when conveying Douglas' instructions to the cameramen, I made sure this was all done well out of Bailey's hearing

A few days later we returned to the site and were joined by the rest of the crew. Two hired Volkswagen Campers had been driven down from London and these served as sleeping accommodation. Douglas and his girlfriend Jean had the luxury of a double bed in the farmhouse. By erecting a tent and screens around the vehicles, the encampment soon became our base. It was soon clear that Douglas had no intention of roughing it in the catering department— no brown rice and tahini for him. A grand hamper from Fortnum's allowed us to sample boars' head pate, smoked salmon and champagne throughout the whole weekend. Whether such decadent goings-on would have met with the approval of the hard core freaks among the crowd was another matter.

Douglas had planned to shoot with three cameras, two mute and one with sound. Any interviews had to be conducted during the day, as we needed to film the bands performing at night. Maintaining any sensible schedule was almost impossible as the interviewees had a habit of not turning up at the appointed time. An attitude of laissez-faire prevailed everywhere, one bordering on the surreal. Such a gross amount of drugs was being consumed, it would have been unlikely to find anyone who was compos-mentis for more than a few minutes at a time. Everywhere was the reek of hashish, and its effects were only too evident when we began filming. Stoned individuals lurched into shot, ruining a take all too frequently. The general ethos—that all was permissible—was beginning to irritate the crew who were intent simply on getting a job done. If I even mildly remonstrated with anyone, I was accused of being uptight, or worse.

"Stay cool, man … everyone's here just to have a far out time, y'know."

"We would just appreciate it if you could wait for a minute, or maybe move over that way a bit …"

"Yeah, I can see where you're at, man … but like … we're just digging what we're into right now, yeah?"

Bailey did not help matters, leaping around mouthing his quasi-profound sentiments. He somehow contrived to get himself into the background of every shot and his stoned grin was everywhere, like some sinister jack-in-the-box. On the occasions when the mask slipped, it was to reveal a permanent sneer which, with his straggly beard, made him resemble a misshapen troll.

To avoid any more frustration with scheduling, Jean took it upon herself to arrange the interviews we needed to film. A brisk manner belying her petite self, she gathered the candidates together on Sunday morning and we filmed them one after the other delivering their spiel. Jean, off-camera with her clipboard, was ready to prompt if they faltered. It was all completed in a few hours which meant we had now only to concentrate on filming the musical performances.

The stage on Saturday night had been taken over by the more prestigious bands, Grid Iron, Oat Willie, and The Yellow Spooks. Lighting was a perennial problem as none of the musicians wished to be blinded by arcs during their performance. We were obliged to keep direct light to a minimum, and were only minimally aided by any lightshow that might be part of an act. On occasions, as the rushes later demonstrated, this gave us some dramatic footage, but much of it was unusable.

We needed to shoot some scenes around the campfires that blazed merrily in one corner of the field. To this end, after filming the bands on Saturday night, I directed one camera to capture this tribal simplicity. Luckily for us, a few recognised bands turned up to play on the Sunday afternoon, the word having spread around the London music scene. This enabled us to get some extra material in the can, and the other two crews to get in amongst the loony dancers. The ubiquitous Bailey could be seen in front of the stage, the more mind-blown individuals cavorting around him like a retinue of demons.

I warned the cameramen not to film too many bare breasts or we could be faced with censorship problems. Sunday turned out to be a very warm day, so it was difficult to avoid the odd nipple in any shot. Douglas seemed pleased with what was being achieved and, thankfully, we had suffered only minor technical problems. If we had been forced to go off site for any reason it would have been a horrendous task. The narrow roads leading to Pillstown had been clogged with motor traffic and crowds of pedestrians from the outset. Their resemblance to ragged refugees was only too apparent to my own eyes.

Douglas called it a wrap late on Sunday afternoon and we began packing up. In the midst of this an unexpected frisson developed. There were only a few stallholders at the festival, it being insisted by Grainey that the event should not be run for profit. As one they were seen to approach Douglas, and it became clear from the raised voices that all was not well. I intervened and quickly discovered that Bailey had extracted sums of money from these entrepreneurs with a promise to name check them in the movie. He had also convinced some wannabe starlets that, in exchange for their favours, they could appear in some of the scenes. It became more and more apparent Bailey had given everyone the impression he was running the production.

While Douglas and I attempted to pacify the stallholders it was discovered that a bag containing some cash had gone missing from Douglas' car. The keys to the vehicle had disappeared at some time during the afternoon and then equally mysteriously reappeared. Jean was convinced they had been taken from her bag. There was nothing for it but to confront Bailey, a move which Douglas reluctantly agreed to do. The outcome was wholly predictable, the suspect protesting his innocence and immediately casting his accusers in the role of villains.

"Why do you wanna bring *me* down, man? That's such a bum scene, giving me all this heavy jive. Where are you at with this bad trip?"

The ranting continued until Douglas and everyone else gave up remonstrating with him. This all left a sour taste. We left the festival with less than cheery memories of the occasion, as if the whole enterprise had been cursed. Quite how much Bailey's malignant influence would affect the production was yet to be revealed.

Having agreed to oversee the editing with Douglas, the technical problems we faced in post now became all too apparent. Much of the sound recording of the bands was of very poor quality, my suggestion to take a feed from the mixing desk having been ignored for some reason. Matching acceptable visuals with usable audio became the worst aspect of a growing nightmare. Despite Jean's efforts, most of the interview footage was unbearably tedious, consisting of platitudes or self-conscious waffling. We were faced with the situation dreaded by every producer—that of trying to save a movie. The editor was not capable of facing the challenge, too often resembling a drowning man going down for the third time. I was blunt with Douglas as to any remedy.

"Our only hope is getting someone who's experienced enough not to run away screaming from all this."

"I totally agree. But do you know anyone?"

"Yes, I do. A guy called Jeff. I don't whether he's around ..."

Douglas assumed an imperious look.

"Do that ... get in touch with him soon as you can."

I was on a mission.

Jeff made himself available and, by an heroic effort, something like a worthwhile film emerged out of the material available. Douglas organised a press screening in London, but it turned out to be a false dawn. The curse of Bailey began to do its evil work. This character had obviously been nursing a considerable resentment against the production and set about making as much trouble for us as possible. He had considerable influence with the underground press, alternative media having some clout in those days, and succeeded in throwing a sizeable spanner in the works. The film was denounced, in holier-than-thou tones on their pages, as not being 'right-on'. Worse still, when approached for comment, Grainey and his cronies proved to be exceptionally craven, joining in with the chorus of condemnation. Anxious to be seen holding the right hippie credentials, they made fatuous statements about 'dodgy vibes' and 'bread-heads'. All this fuelled the fire and guaranteed the movie would be shunned by the audience it was intended for when it eventually appeared.

Times had changed greatly since the heyday of the

Sixties, in a way that was difficult to identify at first. The current 'rock culture', as it was known, reeked of hypocrisy and double-dealing. Its proponents might spout Aquarian principles but were all too eager to adopt Hollywood values of decadence and dishonesty. The rip-off culture was taking over.

With his privileged background Douglas was an easy target for brickbats from the freak community. Though he tried to remain aloof from the brouhaha, it embittered him. He had a genuine zeal for the project and now experienced the indignity of seeing his movie trashed and ignored. In this debacle I did not expect my relationship with Douglas to survive, but miraculously it did so.

4

The telephone outside my door started to jangle just as I was climbing the stairs. I grabbed it and heard my friend Pete's voice. This guy was an enigma in my life, someone I had spoken to frequently but never met in person. He ran an informal agency catering for those who worked in the biz. One day he'd called me asking about my availability and we'd been firm friends ever since. As well as providing such an invaluable service, he had an endless fund of knowledge and always knew the latest gossip. If anyone had his finger in every producer's pie, Pete most certainly did.

"I've been trying to get in touch with you. Been away?"

"In a manner of speaking, yes. On another planet I reckon …"

Pete sounded puzzled, not surprisingly.

"What?"

I hastened to put him back on track.

"Just finished a documentary on the rock festival …"

"Which crew were you with?"

"Douglas … you know, the posh bloke …"

"Right. I heard there were some German guys

filming down there as well ... and some lot from Australia even."

"Don't remember any Germans ... I did meet an Aussie or two ..."

A minor pause.

"You interested in a job on this new historical movie? Shooting starts in three weeks?

"Who's doing it?"

"New outfit ... Amigo Associated Films."

"Christ! Never heard of them ..."

"Me neither ... but it's work ..."

"Absolutely. Buggers can't be choosers."

Pete pressed on.

"Amigo are in partnership with local TV here ... not the BBC ... the other lot."

"Who do I get in touch with?"

"Bloke called Roy Prince ... hang on, I'll give you his number."

I wrote this down carefully on the cover of the phonebook with all the other important numbers, putting a big circle round it.

"What do I go for?"

"Anything you can. It's not a huge set up. If I'd got in touch with you earlier, you could have got AD."

"Never mind. I'll call straight away. Thanks, Pete."

"That's okay, best of luck."

The guys in charge at Amigo gave me the position of assistant to the casting director. To be more accurate I was *assistant* to the assistant casting director. Any fantasies I had about hanging out with celebs, however, went straight out the window on the first day.

The production—*With Fire and Sword*—was a Medieval epic. When I called Pete for a chat he told me only a few of the cast had much of a track-record. The crew were mostly from London, and some local pros had been signed up. They had swiftly divided into two camps, and the director hadn't the personality to unite the differing factions.

Norman, the guy I was assigned to work with, seemed pleasant enough when I called him over the weekend. He quickly explained his brief, to choose background actors from those who answered the cattle call. The only qualification for being a peasant in this version of the Middle Ages was having long hair. Skills of hoeing or husbandry would not be required.

Arriving at the studio at 6 a.m. on Monday morning, I couldn't believe what I saw. It resembled a re-run of the Festival but ten times as chaotic. Although not being an hour I associated with the alternative society, large numbers of the most Neanderthal freaks in the city had gathered in the studio car park. One or two had the Rizlas out already and none too surreptitiously either. Norman was anxiously surveying the scene from behind glass doors in the foyer.

"What am I supposed to do with that bloody lot?"

I stepped in.

"I'll get 'em organised, you pick the ones you want and then get 'em on the coach to the location. I'll send the others home. How's that?"

Norman looked at me as I if I had just uttered great wisdom.

"D'you know … I think that might even work."

Organising the disparate mob into some order so that Norman could inspect them was reasonably straightforward. In weeks to come, the scene would remind me of dockers on the quayside waiting for work. The fortunate candidates having been chosen, they climbed aboard a bus and were taken to a muddy field near the village of Crabley Batch. There, they were required to don rags and old skins before being herded into scenes that required bucolic colour.

After the first week Norman began to regard his charges with blatant contempt, referring to them, often audibly, as 'tossers' and 'idiots'. He should have been more discreet. Word had reached the local chapter of the Hells Angels that hirsute individuals were required and they decided to pay the studio a visit.

The flotilla of bikes arrived en masse on Monday morning, roaring into the car park. The noise must have been heard in the next town. Inside the building Norman put his head in his hands and turned to me with terror in his eyes.

"Why me? Why is it always me who has to face these things? Tell me that."

I had no ready words of consolation. Together we watched the riders dismount and walk over to where our regular actors were grouped. There were shouts of greeting from both sides. I began to walk towards the door. Norman must have feared I was about to abandon him, desperately shouting after me.

"Where you going?"

"Somebody's got to try and sort them out, or we'll have a riot next."

Hesitating at first, Norman made to follow me.

"Looks like we've got one already."

I walked towards the bikers, trying to look as nonchalant as possible. They muttered among themselves and eyed me. It was not difficult to identify their leader. He towered above the rest and had a permanent leer, as well as a scar or two. His name was Panzer.

"Hi. I'm Jack."

Panzer did not stand on ceremony.

"We all looks like stinkin' savages, that's what you want, innit? So we gotta get the part in your movie, like."

I deliberated for a moment.

"Yeah, okay. If you don't mind lining up with everyone else …"

Panzer turned away and spat emphatically on the ground.

"Alright."

"Thanks."

He then addressed the rest of his band.

"You lot! Jack's gonna tell us what to do."

I accompanied him to where everyone had now gathered. For a moment Panzer and I stood together facing the crowd, waiting for Norman. Without warning, this hairy biker suddenly embraced me, at the same time yelling my name to the skies.

"Here he is! He's the fuckin' Jack … Jumpin' Jack Flash."

The mob cheered and roared, and all I could do was smile widely. On the sidelines, I could see Norman staring at us in the most utter amazement.

* * *

Most days, after we had packed the extras off in the coach, there was not a great deal to do. Norman usually shut himself in his office to catch up on paperwork, and I mooched about the TV Studios. I took the opportunity to strike up an acquaintance with anybody involved with production and even those who weren't. From an obliging PA I had even obtained a copy of the screenplay. This was the first time I had examined such a document and was most eager to do so.

Although I was unfamiliar with the format, after I had read the first few pages I could see this was destined to be a turkey even before it took off. The dialogue seemed to have been written by someone waiting for a train, and the plot was so minimal it almost guaranteed the movie would appear lame. This taught me a lot about working in movies. Once the measure of any production was gauged, a 'take the money and run' approach was all that was left. Although I had higher aspirations than being a journeyman in the biz, this was a sobering thought.

The wrap party was held in the Studio's social club. I mingled with those I knew but did not get as much opportunity as I would have liked to hobnob with the director or the producers. Some of the extras had managed to gate crash the occasion and because I had gained a reputation as being more than approachable I was treated like an old friend. Among this crowd were a few girls and although not much of a dancer,

I was soon bopping away happily enough with them.

As the party was breaking up my dancing partner Suzi came closer.

"Do you want to come back to my place?"

"Sounds like a great idea."

Suzi smiled at me mischievously.

"Is it okay if my friend comes with us?"

I nodded, not quite anticipating where this all might lead. I soon found out when the three of us were shedding our clothes in Suzi's bedroom. There was a lot of rolling around together on the bed and we soon got to know each other more than well. Having one woman was pleasant enough—a pair was cream on the cake. I certainly had my cake and ate it too that night.

Student days now seemed a long way off. I was out in the real world and feeling all the better for that. Inevitably, being in Barstowe I knew I would, at some point, run into an old acquaintance or two. Clinton still had an air of intimacy; the place had yet to become the yuppie ghetto it would in the next decade. Although I had never been a fan of Old Boys' Reunions or Alumni Dinners, I was sometimes curious as to the fate of some of my contemporaries. When I ran into Bonzo Hinton in Richardson Gardens one afternoon I was anything but churlish. He and I had been at both school and university together, and I was reasonably eager to compare notes of our doings since those times. We agreed to meet at *The Plum and Wallet* that very evening.

The pub was some way from Clinton, almost on the edge of the city. Rather than attempting any air of sophistication, it was most definitely cosmopolitan. The bar, its low ceiling yellowed with tobacco smoke, spoke of a beery, male ambiance. I recognised Bonzo, already well installed at a table by the window overlooking the street. He was laughing loudly at something he, or someone else, had just said. Next to him was Joe Woods, a tutor at Barstowe University who I had met before at some gathering in Clinton. The other party I did not recognise.

"Hello, Jack. How the devil are you? What are you having?"

Bonzo was about to get up but I waved a restraining hand.

"Don't worry … I'll get this. Anyone else like anything?"

I arrived at the table with a half of lager and another pint for Bonzo. Joe greeted me and the unfamiliar individual introduced himself.

"Roger Thrubb."

Easing myself into a seat opposite Bonzo, I regarded my companions. Tweedy and corduroyed, they represented the kind of blokes who would drift into middle-age without even noticing. Wife, kids and a pot belly would inevitably follow.

"I was just telling Roger and Joe about the last time I saw you … probably at the Uni. Ball."

Bonzo had opted for Law at Barstowe and was now a junior partner with a firm of solicitors in the city; that I knew.

"I'm sure you're right…

"Around five or six years ago. Of course, old Joe here never left … straight from his MA into the Department."

A mild protest.

"I did do my PhD in between …"

"That was just a bit of a holiday up in London though wasn't it … eh, old boy?"

Thrubb seemed to be at a bit of a loss with all this academic chat.

"You clever chaps have one up on me, I was never a student. The old man thought I ought to be off out making money as soon as I left school."

"Probably means you earned a damn sight more than any of us, eh?"

Bonzo poked Thrubb in the ribs as he said this, an annoying habit of his I remembered. Woods turned to me enquiringly.

"Aren't you something to do with films?"

Thrubb looked interested.

"Not an actor?"

"No, no, I'm afraid not … on the production side."

Bonzo quaffed and quipped.

"Another bloody millionaire! Why is it that I always miss the boat, eh?"

Thrubb was consoling.

"All you need is one juicy case, Bonzo, and you can absolutely rake it in. Libel on some big celebrity, that's what you want …"

"Not as easy as all that. It's always the heavyweights up in London who pick up that sort of case."

The reference to the capital prompted Bonzo's next remark.

"You remember Taylor-Jennings don't you, Jack?"

"Sort of ..."

"He's up in town ... along with Chris Potter-Dunbar ..."

After he announced this, not really waiting for any response, I could see Bonzo was looking round intently. He was inspecting the early evening crowd, probably something he did on a regular basis. Chaps obviously popping in for a quick one before going home, a few likely lads, the usual ritual to be seen in any tavern in the kingdom. I wondered what Bonzo was thinking; he was certainly not engaged in looking at the world in the way I always did. He gazed at it and it looked back at him, a reflection of a reflection. All of a sudden I was aware he was off, lurching in the direction of the bar.

"Jack, what you having?"

I told myself I would have one more drink and then head for home.

"One of those bottled Czech lagers ..."

"Fancy stuff, eh? Usual for you chaps?"

And so it went on and probably did in the same way, but in different hostelries, every evening. Bonzo and his drinking buddies, interchangeable, but all of the same ilk. Middle class, on the first few rungs of the ladder in the professions they had chosen, or their parents had chosen for them. Bonzo returned from the bar and almost immediately started examining his watch, prior to looking in my direction.

"Look here, Taylor-Jennings ... Chris Potter-Dunbar ... I was just saying about them ... we've arranged to meet them at *Piper's*."

I didn't say anything, encouraging or otherwise.

"You'll come along won't you, Jack?"

I refused, as politely as I could.

"I'm afraid not. Work to do."

This wasn't exactly true, but I remembered how insistent Bonzo could be, particularly about social engagements. He looked glum but I was firm. The prospect of a lot more waffling and sluicing did not tempt me at all. There was something gloomy about the whole gathering, like some Ibsen play slowly crawling to its predictably dire conclusion. I was sometimes amazed at the way people treated time, how they frittered it away. I regarded every moment as unique, there to be examined closely like a precious jewel.

The rent was due and funds were getting low. Panic hadn't quite set in but I was in a reflective mood over breakfast. The sound of the phone ringing sent me hot foot into the hallway.

"Is that Jack Strange?"

"Certainly is."

"Oh, hi, this is Kelston Films. I believe you know Douglas Hampton?"

"Right, I've worked with him."

"Yeah, that's what he said ... and we have a project here about to start. Would you be interested in the position of Assistant Director on this?"

"Sure ... I think so anyway. When do you start shooting?

"In around two weeks. Is that okay with you? I know it's rather short notice."

"No, that's absolutely fine."

"Probably a twelve week shoot. You'll be paid for that amount of time whatever happens, Douglas made that clear. It'll all be in your contract."

"Can you tell me anything else? About the movie, I mean."

A well-bred laugh greeted the enquiry.

"I don't know an awful lot, personally, except that the location is in Devon."

"Okay."

"But don't worry, I'll post you the address and dates and everything along with your contract. Copy back to me, please …"

"Of course."

"I think we have your address already. It's Clinton in Barstowe isn't it?"

"21 Albert Place. Ground Floor Flat."

"Yes, I've got that … and I've just found the title of the film. Let's see … *A Message for Inspector Stilton*."

She was obviously reading from something in front of her.

"It's adapted from a novel written by … um … Stuart Marsh … that's what it says here."

"Fine. Thanks."

"I'm terribly sorry that's all I know about things, but I think Douglas just wants everyone to turn up at the location. There's a big house, apparently, so there'll be somewhere to stay and everything. Anything else, just ring me up. I'm Philomena, by the way."

"Thanks very much."

"You're welcome. Bye."

Three months work was just what I needed. I also

wanted a little more info about what was I was letting myself in for. And I knew exactly where to go. I called Pete.

"I've just signed up to work with Douglas again …"

Pete paused in deliberation.

"Viscount Hampton … the one with that documentary thing about a rock festival. That died a death didn't it?"

I breathed out, as if to exorcise the memory.

"Certainly did. What do you know about this new one though? *A Message for Inspector Stilton* … I think I got that right."

"I've heard one or two people talking about it … location in the West Country?"

"Somewhere on the Devon coast."

"He's set up a production company to make the movie, along with his two brothers. Kelston Films."

"I wonder who's funding it …"

I had reached the stage when I was as interested in the financial side of production as much as everything else.

"Someone was telling me … I can't remember who … that the whole thing is financed by the trustees of the Earl of Mahogany Estate. It might be some huge tax fiddle, for all I know."

I wondered if that was why Douglas didn't seem particularly bothered about having lost money on the festival film.

"They're right in with an advantage because his family know the BFI people and the Arts Council."

"It's who you know …"

"You can claw a lot of money back that way too … with grants particularly."

I mused.

"Whoever it was I was talking to … someone in the Kelston office, didn't have much idea who was in it or anything."

"Lot of these secretaries and people in Wardour Street don't have a clue … could be a temp."

I paused.

"I wonder why they asked me … apart from my knowing Douglas …"

"Might be because they got let down … who's available … that kind of thing …"

"Maybe that's it."

"When do you start shooting?"

"Middle of March."

"Okay, well good luck. Let me know how it goes."

"I will. Cheers, Pete."

5

Finding out of the way places was not so easy in those days. The arrival of the mobile phone and the Sat. Nav. was some way in the future. Endless country lanes loomed before me. Looking at first quaint, then vaguely sinister, they seemed intent on sending me constantly in the wrong direction. In those days my Ford Escort was not totally reliable either, and anxiety was starting to set in. Finally I spotted a sign in a hedge that proclaimed *Kelston Productions* and breathed several sighs of relief.

A narrow road eventually joined a drive that led to a large stone house overlooking the sea. I parked next to some other cars, all looking smarter than mine. After unloading my bags, I went in search of Douglas. I didn't have to look very far; he was standing at the entrance to the house as if he owned it. I would have to ask someone if he actually did.

Since I had last seen Douglas I heard he had been involved in various film projects. How much commitment, financial or executive, had been required from him, I didn't know. Rumours, away from Pete's more discreet circuit, were more waspish. They usually went like this—Douglas was a randy old roué who had only got into the biz in order to exercise the ferret. I was in no position to judge the truth of such scandalous innuendo as his social circle and mine, such as it was, did not overlap.

The dashing moustache and twinkling eyes remained, but he had a different air. Gone were the hippy trinkets and Moroccan shoulder bag. Hair styled in Kensington High St. and what looked like an Yves St. Laurent jacket outwardly proclaimed the change. Douglas had obviously decided, like many others at this time, that the way-out ethos should be permanently returned to Bohemia. I had heard that the perfume of hashish now hardly ever intruded in hip circles. Cocaine was the preferred drug and the crunching of Bolivian rocks could be heard constantly in Sloane Square.

Douglas waved in friendly fashion and I noted the unmistakeable bearing—the same that would once have inspired the troops, before they lined up to be slaughtered by the enemy.

"Hi. How's it going?"

"Fine, bit of a struggle to get here."

Douglas' smile was even wider than before.

"Right, it is a bit out of the way."

Before I could say any more a gofer appeared out of nowhere and led me into the house. The ground floor was obviously where things happened, the paraphernalia of filming being everywhere. Upstairs I was shown into a large communal bedroom, the sort of accommodation I had been prepared for. I dumped my stuff on one of the beds as I was informed when we would eat and where I could find the director.

* * *

I knew Gary was a veteran of several features, nothing mega successful, but sound, mid-range efforts that always returned their investment. A neat, compact figure, he radiated a combination of efficiency and anxiety familiar in the film world. Gary took me on a brief tour of the three main sets, interiors dressed to look like a typical Agatha Christie scenario. Such was the style Douglas and the designer were obviously seeking to emulate.

As we were chatting, we were joined by a moustachioed stocky type in his mid-forties. Phil was the cameraman, still retaining a modicum of jollity despite his long-suffering demeanour. He was complaining to Gary that some of his gear had not yet arrived.

"You would have thought putting a couple of mobile trucks in a van and bringing them down from London wasn't that difficult, wouldn't you?"

Gary was conciliatory.

"No sign of anything yet?"

"I was *assured* by Kelston *everything* would be here for when I turned up. Amazing isn't it?"

"We can get by tomorrow, even Tuesday, with what we've got, Phil. Can you call 'em again? Get Tommy to do it in the morning."

"That prat! Calls himself a line producer! He couldn't even *draw a straight line* …"

He went off grumbling. Gary smiled, but only briefly.

"The organisation is a bit less than ideal in some areas here, as you'll soon find out."

This sounded ominous for some reason, as if I

wasn't being told the whole story. I looked enquiringly at Gary.

"One of the problems is that Mike … our dearly loved co-producer … is a nice chap but doesn't exactly assert himself."

I nodded understandingly and Gary continued.

"It's always a lot better when you've got a production team who are buzzing about checking that everything's up together all the time."

I found myself asking questions without realising it.

"Is this is a much a smaller production than you're used to …"

Gary smiled.

"You've been doing some research on me I can tell."

"Impressed by your track record that's all …"

He smiled at this blatant flattery, as I hoped he would.

"The movies I've done so far have been a bit more *grand* that's true … but there we are."

I thought it wise not to make any more comments at this point, just appear involved.

"So, what's happening?"

"Tomorrow morning? We won't be doing anything terribly clever. I really want everyone to get used to the sets, so we'll go through blocking and lighting on Set One, and do a bit of rehearsal. You okay with handling actors?"

"Yeah, I think so."

"They're young … pretty well all of them … so they've got their little ways."

I could see Gary thinking and planning, as every director does constantly.

"Might get you to do some second unit stuff too …"

"Fine."

"We'll lead you in gently …"

Gary looked a mite serious.

"A twelve week shoot sounds like we've got bags of time, but I really do want to crack on with it all, just in case …"

"Problems …"

Gary looked at me somewhat sharply.

"There's always problems … it's the ones that shouldn't happen I don't like."

I wondered about this as we made our way to where we were to have dinner. A certain air of foreboding hung over everything, one that could not be sensibly ignored.

I hadn't been involved with any communal living since I was a student, and it took some readjusting to the regime. Not so much listening to the sound of someone snoring, or the queue for the bathroom in the morning, more getting used to being with other people 24/7. In the coming weeks I would regularly take walks along the coastal path whenever I could. The relative wildness of the coast, where the elements inevitably ruled, gave me a break from anything that was happening on set. Making a feature, even as AD, was a more intense experience than I had realised.

Douglas was hardly in evidence at all during the first week. I would have liked to renew our acquaintance but I deliberately stayed away from his room. He seemed to spend a lot of time there ensconced with Elizabeth, his new girlfriend. Jean had obviously disappeared from the picture but, if the rumours of his many amours were true, that was hardly surprising. Elizabeth was nominally in charge of the catering, which seemed a convenient arrangement for the Viscount. That way all his physical needs could be satisfied by the same firm.

Daily meetings between Douglas and Gary, to which I had yet to be invited, were ongoing. I got plenty of experience with the nuts and bolts of filming, and by the end of Week 2 Gary and I had adopted a routine. We would discuss the next day's shooting each evening, after which we would sometimes arrange to switch roles. That way we kept things fresh for the cast. Sometimes I did the blocking before handing the actors over to Gary, at other times I was in charge of rehearsal. The process of lighting the set gradually became less arcane, and I was getting more familiar with the sound man's role. I was learning fast.

In an annexe to the main house was the communal lounge. Being far enough away from the sets there was thus no problem with unwanted sound. Unfortunately, the room had been virtually taken over by Tommy Box, Douglas' shadow. My first impression may have been tainted by Phil's outburst, but he turned out to be an even more nauseous than I had anticipated. A squat object with a pageboy haircut, he could have easily played the part of a pantomime dame. He reminded me of the odious Bailey, and I wondered if Douglas always featured some sort of jester in his entourage.

Tommy had an extremely attractive girlfriend—Barbara—who was permanently perched on the arm of his chair, showing off her legs. It would have been beyond the wit of man to find any reason why she had attached herself to this excrescence. Even her many attractions could not bring me to spend time in the lounge, and thereafter I hid in the props store with a book. Without willing it I had become as elusive a figure as Douglas himself.

The next evening, as I was embarking on my usual stroll, I encountered Elizabeth. I introduced myself and she seemed friendly enough, appearing to be genuinely concerned about my welfare.

"I do hope everybody's warm enough at night, it can get awfully chilly down here."

I hastened to reassure her I would not perish from hyperthermia.

"And you're okay with the meals?"

"Yes, lovely …"

At that moment Douglas appeared, wearing a cloth cap. If his intention was to appear egalitarian, it was not a convincing pose. I was aware his patrician attitude on set had already caused some resentment, sowing the seeds for the series of contretemps that would later occur. He briefly greeted me before firmly leading Elizabeth away. I was slightly baffled by his behaviour. Still musing on this, I was about to set off once more when someone else appeared from the house.

"Hi."

"Hello, Mike."

"Everything okay with you? I haven't had much chance to have a chat … been a bit rushed off my feet."

I thought this was a bit far-fetched as a resume of his role but merely commented on business in hand.

"Gary seems to be arranging things so we can get the most out of a day. He seems to think we need to get as many set–ups done as we can."

Mike seemed surprised to hear this, as if the actual process of filming was something alien to him.

"Oh, right … yeah."

His vagueness was in keeping with his horn-rims and schoolmasterly manner, which I found slightly disconcerting. Maybe I wasn't used to production crew looking like Mr. Chips.

"How are these production meetings going?"

"Oh, I don't actually get to go to many of those …"

I continued to marvel at the feudalism that seemed to be rampant in the organisation.

"I see."

Mike looked at me even more abstractedly.

"If you ever fancy a drink one night, there's a pub just a little way along the main road … *The Hunter and Hounds*."

"That's good to know."

Mike started to wander off.

"I'll see you around."

I looked out to sea. The horizon above the opposite coast looked less than inviting and I abandoned any ideas of a constitutional.

* * *

As Gary was satisfied with progress on the interiors we decided to shoot some scenes on the beach. This meant an early start and what promised to be a long day. We had to be ready to film before dawn, which meant getting up several hours before the sun rose. Manhandling a lot of gear in the dark down the narrow path which led to the shore inevitably prompted a fair amount of grumbling and cursing. Tempers were frayed even before we began filming. Phil was particularly tetchy as the camera equipment decided to be temperamental, and an essential piece of equipment had been left behind at the house. I could see the gofers were going to be kept busy most of the day.

Starting the generator for the lights proved to be beyond the sparks' capabilities. Gary had just decided to make do with natural light when it finally coughed into life. By this time the sun had appeared and, if we wanted to catch the morning light, blocking and rehearsal would have to be virtually ignored in favour of shooting straight away. The actors were cold and stiff from sitting around waiting to begin, and getting any animation going from them was not easy for Gary. It took a few takes before we could get into a rhythm that was not forced, but eventually we did.

Our next concern was a bit more basic, we were hungry. Phil, being the man he was, voiced the general view.

"I could kill for a bacon sandwich."

Everyone started looking at Mike.

"I did remind Elizabeth last night we needed to have breakfast prepared and brought down. It should have been here by now."

But it wasn't, and there was nothing for it but to send a gofer back to the house to find out why. Gary shot one more scene and then we waited. After nearly an hour, two figures could be seen approaching down the path. As they drew closer they were revealed as Douglas and Elizabeth. It could be clearly seen neither of them were carrying anything that resembled anything like breakfast. A groan went up. Whether aware of this or not, Douglas was hot with anger when he came onto the shore.

"What's all this hassle about then? Demanding Elizabeth make special meals!"

Mike spoke up hesitatingly.

"I arranged with Elizabeth that breakfast would be brought to us, as we had to start shooting early ..."

Douglas crashed his foot on the pebbles.

"If you want meals at different times than usual, make your own bloody arrangements! You can't expect us to run around after you."

For her part, Elizabeth looked embarrassed and flushed. I suspected Douglas, whose sexual demands had become quite legendary, had insisted on the usual morning bout of prolonged lovemaking. Elizabeth had been confined *ipso facto* between the sheets, unable to attend to any catering duties. There was an awkward silence broken by Phil's curt comment.

"I bet *you've* made sure you've had *your* fucking breakfast."

Douglas glowered, and the atmosphere was ripe for a confrontation. Realising this only too well, Gary stepped in.

"It's okay. It's probably time for a break anyway. We'll go back up to the house, have an early lunch and get back to Set 1 this afternoon."

Elizabeth was obviously relieved by Gary's diplomacy and started back up the path. Although still obviously angry, Douglas followed her. One of the gofers began to dismantle the lights, and Phil was packing up his own gear. Gary took me aside.

"That sort of thing shouldn't happen! Why was he like that about a perfectly straight-forward arrangement? He'd have a strike on his hands on some sets if he carried on like that. It's ridiculous."

I pondered.

"Douglas does act rather strangely, as if he's not part of the movie at all."

Gary was short.

"He'd better not upset Phil too much. He's an amazing cameraman, but he's also got an amazing temper."

From the beginning I had been puzzled by the screenplay. In rehearsal, all the cast had stumbled over the dialogue at some point. Sometimes they even fell flat on their faces. The problem was not with their acting ability but the actual words they were expected to deliver. I decided to spend one evening really studying the screenplay and making notes. It was a depressing experience; the writing was nearly as bad as that for the historical epic. I had a lot of sympathy for Gary, who was attempting to make a reasonable film out of such difficult material.

Even from my own limited perspective, the faults

in the composition were glaringly obvious. Whoever had been commissioned to adapt the novel obviously had very little experience in that field. I was certain the bulk of the lines were merely an exposition of the book's narrative, resulting in a collection of clumsy, interminable speeches. There had been no attempt at editing the text of the novel so as to make it more filmic. I could see trouble ahead, not just for Gary as the director, but for the cast to put life into such a sterile text. A taste of the kind of conflict that lay in the future was made evident the next day.

Presumably taking his cue from Douglas, Tommy had a habit of appearing on the set, usually during a take. If this was not disruptive enough, he often smoked too. In those days, cigarettes were still socially acceptable, but passing round a joint was definitely going too far, in my view. Martin, who played a rebellious character in the film, was always ready for a blast, and this encouraged others to indulge. Performances did not markedly improve after such episodes. On one of the rare occasions I saw Douglas I mentioned this, but he was almost dismissive of my complaint.

The rift between him and the company widened almost daily and was to do so even more. During a scene the next day matters came to a head. Eve and Roz featured in a scene where they were arguing over the merits of Martin's character. This had been difficult enough to achieve in rehearsal. The script offered little clue as to any real motivation and the actors were left in the dark. After several takes, Gary was still not satisfied, almost at a complete loss. Without warning,

Douglas stepped in and proceeded to address the two girls.

"If you play it like that it's never going to work ..."

Eve, already upset and confused, reacted badly to this. She was obviously holding back the tears.

"I'm doing my best!"

"Well, it's not good enough."

I was convinced Gary would step in at this point, but he seemed too stunned to intervene. The next moment the inevitable happened and Eve rushed off the set crying profusely. There was a terrible silence. It was broken by Phil stepping away from the camera and, obviously addressing Douglas, having his say.

"That's a lot of fucking help then, isn't it, mate!"

Gary threw his hands in the air and all was confusion. Douglas seemed oblivious to the frisson he had caused and simply walked off, Tommy trailing along behind him.

The atmosphere was leaden at dinner, with conversation about as sparkling as a votive candle. I ate what was on offer and set off to drive to *The Hunter and Hounds*. Wanting to get away from the house and assess the situation was essential for my peace of mind. When I got there, the pub didn't look as if it attracted much custom outside the holiday season. Only one other vehicle was in the car park.

The bar was how I expected it to be—kitted out for the tourists with warming pans, sabres, and muskets on the walls. Recognising one of the cast in a corner, I waved in friendly fashion. The gesture was vaguely returned. The landlord didn't seem to care whether

I was there or not, but someone else did. On a stool, ferociously studying his pint, was Gary.

"Hi, not disturbing you I hope?"

"No, that's fine."

I ordered a bottled lager for myself and we sipped in silence. The landlord returned to reading the paper.

"So, how's it all going then?"

This was meant as a throwaway remark but Gary took it as an excuse to unburden himself—*in excelsis*.

"Frankly, mate, I don't know how we're going to get through this, or rather how *I'm* going to get through it."

Knowing this might be a marathon discussion, I edged in carefully.

"I must admit I did read the script …"

Gary was quick to respond.

"Total and absolute crap! I'm damn sure Doug knows it is, but he won't admit it. Some friend of his father's wrote the original novel … which isn't very good anyway … and the screenplay is even worse. It was a disaster before we even started."

"I wonder you took it on …"

Gary shook his head morosely.

"Why do we ever take anything on? I was trying to decide whether to do Doug's project or something else … that seemed to be taking an age to come together so I went for his."

I nodded sympathetically.

"Trouble was I agreed to do it without really looking at the screenplay … and when I *did* I thought it would be okay. I rang Doug and said I could do a reasonable job … but only if I was given a totally free hand."

From today's showing, that proviso had not been adhered to.

"Douglas isn't being terribly helpful …"

"You can say that again, and I'm not just talking about the *incidents* we've had so far."

"No?"

"He's got a habit of *having a chat* to the actors after we've finished for the day too. They're knackered and want to get their makeup off and shower … the last thing they want is one of his little lectures."

I was taken aback.

"Surely he shouldn't be doing that …"

"Lot of things he ought not to be doing … but unfortunately he does. *Fait accompli.*"

Gary was looking at me fixedly.

"Did you ever wonder why you got the AD job at the last minute?"

"I did rather, yes."

"The guy they had lined up, as soon as he heard Doug was involved didn't want to know and quit."

This was a bit of a facer.

"Is that true?"

"Better you know that now, rather than thinking we're all jolly pals together. Pretty well everyone is totally pissed off … and big time … I can tell you that."

"Our cameraman doesn't seem to be a very happy bunny."

Gary put down his pint.

"What Doug doesn't realise is just how good Phil is … or how lucky we are to have him."

"He certainly knows his stuff … I mean … just

from the rushes …"

Gary looked despondent once more.

"I've tried to you keep you out of the way of all this, y'know."

"I appreciate that. Thanks."

The landlord looked up from his paper to see if refills were required. They were.

"These meetings we've been having …"

"What goes on at those?"

"Mostly, it's Doug making some ridiculous suggestion, and me having to tell him why it won't work. Mike doesn't actually say anything, of course."

"No, I can imagine."

Gary shrugged.

"I know Doug pretty well. We were at Cambridge together, and basically he's a nice enough bloke. Why he wanted to get involved in *films* I just can't understand."

I pondered the more while the landlord set down our drinks.

"How does Elizabeth fit into all this?"

"She just goes along with whatever he says. That's the other thing … nobody will stand up to him. I just find it such hard work discussing anything with him, I've more or less given up."

I reflected on this while taking in the line of pewter pots above our heads, each one lovingly engraved with the owner's name.

"And where's the funding coming from?"

"The Estate … nowhere else. The trustees gave the Earl the go-ahead, though I think the BFI have put some of their own investment in there."

I thought of what Pete had said.

"He's producer and exec. And his brothers are co-execs. Talk about keeping it in the family."

"And this Tommy …"

Gary's eyes went skyward.

"He's got his fingers in there somewhere. Again … I don't know how or why."

"I wouldn't trust that guy to tell me the right time."

"I agree."

"How do the cast feel, d'you think?"

"Well, the girls are just keen to please, but Mart is really fed up and I'm not surprised. He's the lead, and his lines are the worst written of the lot. Any direction in the screenplay is pretty well non-existent … so I've got to try and make some sense of everything all the time."

At that moment the silent figure in the corner got up and came over to us. He had the studied air of someone who is extremely drunk but determined not to show it. Gary looked slightly wary. The actor held out his hand to me.

"Colonel Fanshawe."

I didn't say anything.

"Well, I'm not really him … just my character … one tends to forget one's own name after a time. So whoever it is today … that'll do."

"Sounds about right."

The actor studiously avoided looking at either myself or Gary.

"I'm trying to perfect a method of drinking so that I can have a lot but not get tight … or fat. So far I haven't succeeded. I may have to do a lot more research."

Gary and I exchanged glances but did not comment. There was really nothing to say.

Because she was attached to Tommy, I had wrongly dismissed Barbara as a gold digger, or a bimbo. On one of those rare occasions when I went into the communal room she was there on her own. We got talking and I quickly realised she was not only pleasant to talk to, but also extremely perceptive.

"Do you live in London?"

"No, in Barstowe ..."

"You don't know anyone who wants a flat in Fulham do you?"

I was alert.

"It belongs to my sister. It's incredibly cheap and very nice ... furnished too."

There followed one of those moments that determines our destiny. Without really knowing why, I decided I wanted to move to London. I could have said that it would further my career but that wouldn't have been entirely true. At that moment Wardour St. was almost a spent force as the centre of the biz.

"I'll have it ..."

"Oh, really? Wow ... great."

She smiled, as if admiring my enterprise, or maybe she just liked me. I didn't have time to decide about any subtlety like that as Tommy chose that moment to come into the room. Did he scowl at me for having the temerity to speak to his woman? Probably. I didn't really care.

By the beginning of Week 5 the atmosphere was so tense whenever Douglas showed his face on set that a major ruckus was almost inevitable. Ironically, when it did happen some days later, it was during a romantic interlude in the story. The audience knows that Eve is two-timing Martin's character. He suspects, but is too in love with her to bring about a confrontation. I had run through the whole sequence in rehearsal and was confident we could go for a take. Gary agreed and, after a final run through, we got set up. A dolly shot that came in for a tight close up on Martin and Eve was the crucial element for the crew. I had just called 'action', when another voice was heard, insistent and hectoring.

"Wait a minute! Hang on!"

I couldn't believe what was happening, and I don't think anyone else could either. Douglas simply strode onto the set and halted proceedings. What he actually wanted to say—some trivial detail about costume or lightning—wasn't important. He had completely ruined the take and, in terms of movie etiquette, it was unforgivable. It was an unwritten rule that only an earthquake or a fire was permitted to bring filming to a halt. Gary was ashen faced and stared at Douglas open-mouthed. A long second elapsed before Martin, who was obviously completely thrown, walked off the set, Eve following him. Gary could only just get his words out.

"I'm calling a break. If everyone could be back in an hour, please."

What happened next was quite extraordinary. The entire crew simply melted away and Douglas was left alone on the set. I glanced at him briefly as I departed, but it was impossible to know what was going through his mind at that moment. His expression was set and determined.

Assuming Martin and Eve had retired to their dressing room, I decided my place was with Gary and sought him out. I could not find him anywhere inside the house, and eventually came upon him occupying a bench positioned with a view out to sea. I sat down beside him, determined not to speak until he did.

"What the fuck was he doing?"

"Pretty strange behaviour, I must admit."

"That was a tricky enough shot to block and light anyway … plus the rehearsal … which I thought you did very well by the way …"

"Thanks."

Gary put his head in his hands.

"… and he just goes and screws it all up. Just like that."

This was the final straw and I dreaded what I knew was bound to happen next.

Gary was not prepared to film anymore that day and I supported his decision. I was convinced it would have been impossible to prise Martin and Eve out of the dressing room to go through the scene again. At dinner it was almost as if a vow of silence had been taken by everyone present. When I peeked into the communal lounge that was noticeably empty too. Feeling unsettled and not knowing quite what to do, I wandered into the car park. There I found Gary sucking feverishly on a cigarette. He threw it on the ground as soon as he saw me.

"I didn't know you smoked ..."

"I don't ... usually."

We stood together in silence, both of us probably occupied with the same thoughts. Our reverie was interrupted by the sound of a Volkswagen van coming up the drive. The puttering tone of the engine, a ubiquitous sound in those days, insistently demanded attention. The vehicle halted and after much slamming of doors two figures emerged. Although they passed close by us, neither spoke. They strode purposefully into the house and were gone. I looked enquiringly at Gary.

"Who are they?"

Gary paused before making any reply.

"That's the two brothers ... Gorringe and Grindley ... obviously Doug has felt the need to call in reinforcements."

The showdown came on Friday morning. It was impossible for Douglas to ignore what was now virtually open rebellion, and he told Mike to summon cast and crew to the lounge. When he made his entrance, accompanied by Elizabeth and his two brothers, the sight resembled some perverse state occasion. While everyone else was seated, they chose to line up along one wall. Phil was perched in an alcove, as if ready to defend his territory against all comers. Douglas advanced into the room and spoke amicably enough—at first.

"Obviously we've got one or two problems here and I'd like them brought out into the open. I want all this sorted out."

Martin, voted spokesman for the cast, started off, as someone making a reasonable complaint.

"It really is such a shitty script, that's what it comes down to. The story doesn't go anywhere and the lines are just dreadful. It's almost impossible for any of us to learn stuff like that and trying to say it on camera is even worse."

Douglas didn't respond, just looked fixedly at him for an instant.

"Okay, that's one thing. Anyone else got anything to say?"

Phil could not disguise his irritation. He bluntly pointed out that Douglas' behaviour so far during the filming had been unprofessional and, in his view, unforgiveable.

"There should be one person on set saying what goes on … that's *the director* … that's why he's called that. No one else has any right to interfere, you, or anyone else."

Douglas bristled, and looked like he might have something equally forthright to say in return. Phil, however, had not quite finished.

"I've worked on films for more than twenty years

and I've never come across this sort of thing before. It's all total bollocks."

A heavy silence followed. The ball was in Douglas' court and we all waited for his return service. An apology would have been the most tactical response, or at the very least some sort of explanation. He did neither. I noticed his moustache had started quivering. When he spoke, his voice was so clipped it sounded like a recorded message.

"First of all, I don't agree at all with you, Martin. It's certainly not a *shitty script*, not at all. It's a perfectly good adaption of a very good novel."

Nobody said anything, giving Douglas the chance to come in with the old one—two.

"Maybe the real answer is to make some changes in the cast rather than the script."

This was fighting talk and a few of the young things gasped in surprise. Phil, however, was not to be intimidated.

"You carry on like that, chum, and you'll be looking for a new crew as well as a cast, I can tell you that."

Before Douglas could reply, Gary spoke up. He obviously felt uneasy about crossing swords with Douglas, someone he regarded as a friend, and his voice trembled.

"I'd like to say that, as the director on this movie, I couldn't wish for a better cast and crew … always hardworking … dedicated. We should be very grateful we've got them, Doug. More important, is that every day we *are* fighting against an inadequate script and Martin is absolutely right."

Determined not to stand on the sidelines, I spoke up too.

"On that, I'd like to say that I did study the screenplay in detail myself, and it definitely *is* full of holes … clunky and unconvincing. Rehearsals have been trying, to say the least and certainly not through the fault of any of the actors."

Douglas evidently hadn't been prepared for such a united front. He obviously wasn't used to having his authority questioned either. His Crusader persona was suddenly evoked, as if he was about to lead his knights in a charge, riding down any who stood in his way. His voice cracked when he spoke—harsh and unforgiving.

"You all listen to me! This is my movie and I have every right to say what I want, whenever I want. I don't care what anyone here thinks about that either, you can all take it or leave it."

As he said this, the two brothers took up a position one on each side of him, looking remarkably like cartoon heavies. What stopped the spectacle being sinister was its bizarre element. Feelings were certainly running high, too much so for Elizabeth who chose that moment to walk out of the room. Douglas glared about him for a moment before following her, along with his henchmen. The silence that followed was extraordinary, one eventually broken by Phil's voice.

"That's that then … end of story."

Somehow I was convinced the situation could be saved, and I spoke up in a voice louder than I intended.

"No! Whatever happens, it's up to us … everyone

here … we've got to finish the movie."

To my surprise, there was unanimous agreement. For a moment I thought everyone was going to start cheering. Martin and Eve were beaming at me, and Gary and Mike were nodding their heads vehemently. After a moment or two Phil joined in. We were united and we would stay that way until the end of the shoot.

Barbara had agreed to meet me at her sister's flat on Saturday morning so I could sign the lease and pick up the keys. I explained this to Gary as soon as I was able to.

"This is all a bit full-on having to go to London, right now, I know … but I do have to sign the lease on this flat."

"That's fine, go ahead."

"I'll be back tomorrow evening … we can spend all Sunday deciding what we're going to do, if you like."

He was smiling and spontaneously shook me by the hand.

"Thanks again, Jack, for what you said in there. I rather think that saved the day."

"Had to be done, the show must go on."

Gary smiled. It was the first time I had seen him do that for some time.

The flat was in Bronsart Rd. not far from the Fulham Palace Cemetery, a useful landmark if nothing else. Fearing London traffic was going to be heavy, I set off early. I arrived at noon with time to spare. Barbara was waiting for me and looking, if that were possible, even more gorgeous than I remembered. Her skirt was so short, the neckline so low, that the two could have met without any obvious effort at all.

"Hi. Isn't this exciting?"

"Seeing you again is too."

Used to men flirting with her, I was sure, Barbara pouted in a practised way. I followed her down the area steps and through the front door. Although a basement flat, it was light and welcoming. The sitting room led out into a walled garden at the back. Forsythia and daffodils were already making an appearance.

"Great."

"Glad you like it … the last people were very good and looked after everything so nicely."

I noticed the phone on a table.

"That's handy."

"Yeah. We can sort all that out, and the bills. Lucy is in South America so we'll have to get you to pay everything into her bank account here. Is that alright?"

"Of course."

"Great. Let me show you the bedroom."

There was a double bed which took up most of the room. Barbara immediately went and sat on it.

"Comfy."

"Looks like it."

If she had lain on it, with her long legs stretched out invitingly I would have been in with more than a chance. She got up off the bed in double-quick time, however, and put her arms round my neck, kissing me gently on the cheek.

"Let's save that little treat for another day, yeah?"

"Promise?"

"Oh, yes. I never break a promise."

I looked at her eyes and lips and decided she was the most gorgeous creature I had ever seen in my life. Gently she drew away. I returned to the ordinary world, with some reluctance.

"Did you know there was some trouble with the movie?"

She was casual.

"Yeah, I did. I've been up here most of this week. Tommy phoned me yesterday after it all happened."

"Did he say anything about it?"

Barbara shook her head perfunctorily.

"Not really, except that he and Douglas ... and Elizabeth presumably ... were leaving."

I must have shown my surprise.

"Is that right? Where have they gone?"

"I don't know ... probably up to Mahogany House. Tommy spends a lot of time up there anyway ... he lives in one of the Lodges."

"That's incredible."

Barbara smiled.

"What? To just push off like that?"

"Well, yes ..."

"I don't know. Douglas is like that, I think. All guys are just a little crazy anyway, aren't they?"

I had certainly met some in my life who had been more than a little insane, that was true.

When I returned to the house knowing what I did, I would have been surprised to have seen Douglas' car in the car park. There was no sign of the brothers' Volkswagen van either. When I opened the front door I sensed something was very different too.

I found Gary in what had been Douglas' room— the production office. He was having a frank and meaningful exchange with Mike. The latter had his usual abstracted air which, combined with a certain anxiety, gave him a unique aura. I sat down in the nearest chair and awaited developments.

"Basically, Mike, you've got to get in touch with Kelston on Monday … first thing … and find out what's going on."

"Right, right, I'll do that."

"They may not know anything about this, of course, Douglas may not have even told them … but somebody there must know something by now."

Phil came in, nodded to me, and took up a position facing Mike.

"Did Doug say anything to you … *anything at all* … before he buggered off?"

"He just said they were all going back to London because there were things he had to sort out."

Gary intervened.

"He didn't say *when* he was going to be in touch at all?"

"No. He did seem to be in a bit of hurry to get away."

Gary indicated the litter of papers abandoned on the desk.

"Will any of this stuff mean anything to you, Mike?"

"It might, I haven't really …"

Phil butted in.

"Look, mate, we're not trying to give you a hard time, we just want to know a few things. If Douglas isn't prepared to speak to any of us, then you're going to have to be the go-between."

Mike obviously felt he had to defend Douglas, even perfunctorily.

"I'm sure Douglas will be reasonable about everything …"

Phil replied sharply.

"He hasn't been very reasonable so far! Leaving us all in the lurch like that. What's going to happen about catering … for a start?"

Gary looked up and smiled, knowing Phil's ongoing concern about his stomach.

"I'm sure we can sort that out ourselves. I'm more worried about everyone getting paid."

Mike began muttering, none too coherently.

"I'm sure that will all been taken care of too."

Gary looked hard at him.

"You're sure of that?"

"I'm just sure Douglas won't let us down."

Phil shook his head.

"I'm not sure I can trust a bloke who just walks out on everyone and doesn't even say why."

Gary stood up.

"There's no point in wondering about what might, or might not, happen. When Mike rings the office we should have some idea at least. I don't think we should do any more shooting until that's been done."

Phil nodded.

"I'm all for finishing the movie but we've got to

know where we stand first."

And that was how it was left for the moment.

Around noon on Monday Mike, looking more than awkward, took the floor in the lounge.

"First of all … I've spoken to Douglas and everyone's contract will be honoured …"

Some muted applause greeted this, cut short by one of the lighting crew.

"We'll need transport out with all this hired gear later on. Does Kelston know what's happening about that?"

"I did ask, they said the firm only need twenty-four hours' notice and then they'll turn up."

"Fair enough."

Mike looked around ready for more questions. There weren't any. He took a breath.

"I told Douglas we planned to finish the movie … he said he was sorry he couldn't be there to see it."

Inevitably, this got a raucous response and to save Mike's blushes, Gary stepped forward.

"Okay. Thanks Mike, for sorting all that out. That's really appreciated."

With obvious relief, Mike stepped out of the limelight.

"Now we're back in business, what I'd like to do is this … I figure we can finish shooting by Friday … but it will mean a few long days."

Gary pressed on.

"I'd really like to shoot today if that's okay with you all. Every little bit of time is going to help right now. If cast and crew can be on Set 1 and Set 2 in an hour ... we'll shoot with two crews. Some of you who previously have had lowly occupations may find yourselves promoted."

There were ribald shouts of 'About time!' from the gofers.

Gary, Phil and I gathered once more in the production office. Mike joined us for the war council. He had definitely changed, and the crisis had evoked a new spirit in all of us. I was really looking forward to the filming. Gary was obviously thinking about all manner of things at the same time.

"What will happen about the sets when we've finished?"

Phil was quick to reassure him on that one.

"Get Kelston to notify the carpenters for Thursday, if we know we're going to wrap on Friday. They'll take everything down and get shot of it, work all night if they have to, you see. Those blokes work like ... no, I won't say it."

Despite himself Gary grinned.

"That'll still give us time to do some exteriors on Friday ... that's what I thought."

Predictably, Phil was on the case in another department.

"*What are we going to do about this catering?*"

Mike stepped in.

"There was only ever Elizabeth and the two local girls ... they turned up today and just carried on, that's how everyone got breakfast. There's enough stuff here to keep us going till Friday."

Phil looked wistful.

"Ah, yes breakfast ... a distant memory ..."

"They've organised sandwiches for lunch."

"Bacon?"

Gary eyed him.

"Do you ever think about anything else than food?"

Phil was equal to this.

"Since my missus pushed off with that boom bloke I haven't had a lot of the other."

Gary returned to Mike.

"And what happens next Saturday?"

"Douglas asked me to close up the house and give the key back to the estate agents."

Phil looked quizzical.

"Post-production?"

Mike shrugged.

"All I can do is take the cans to the office."

With that, the meeting was over. Gary made a move to go downstairs.

"I'm going to sort out Set 1 ready for blocking."

Phil was close behind him.

"We'll have to divide the lights. What's going to happen about sound?"

"Shoot mute on 2. Can you handle directing, Jack?"

I said I could, and I meant it.

With Gary now completely in charge there was more than a sparkle in the air—the joint was jumping. After we had both blocked our respective scenes, I took him aside.

"I can handle both rehearsals as well if you

want …"

"That would be good. I really do need to sort this lighting out with Phil. What will happen on Set 2 is a bit more straightforward I think."

"Yeah, I can make do with key and fill."

I tapped the script I was holding.

"Listen, I reckon we can afford to cut some of this …"

"I think we're going to have to."

"If I go through it tonight, and show you what I've done tomorrow first thing, then we'll be sorted for the rest of the week."

"Brilliant. We can almost improvise the takes we need today."

Now I knew we were really cooking and, by Thursday, we had gained enough time to put down dolly tracks for a major exterior. These were the days before the steadicam had come into its own, and there was little alternative when a tracking shot was needed. Gary wanted to use natural light for the scene so we shot in the hour before sunset, and then kept the tracks down to shoot a night scene after the sun had set. This meant really tight rehearsals, so as to minimise the takes. Martin and Eve were ultra-professional with hardly any fluffs at all.

There was very little else for Phil to do apart from a few cutaways and some scenic fills. Talk turned towards having our own wrap party. Mike was deputised to approach the landlord of *The Hunter and Hounds* and arrange something for Saturday evening.

* * *

The landlord provided a makeshift karaoke and we clowned around in the bar, consuming more cider than was good for us. Mike had ferried what remained of the stores to the pub so there were enough snacks to satisfy even Phil. Over the years I would attend more grand affairs than this after a shoot, but none so much from the heart.

Lusting after the girls on set hadn't been on my agenda during the shoot. With all the hassles they had endured I felt more protective toward them than anything else. Tonight, however, I was feeling relaxed and not a little randy. The party having reached the most swinging it would get, I had stepped outside to get some air. When Roz appeared out of nowhere I was definitely interested. She was wearing a skimpy top and long sweater which also did service as a skirt.

"Hiya. You okay?"

I leant back on the bench where I was sitting.

"Yeah, I'm fine."

Roz sat down beside me and moved closer, as I rather hoped she would. I put my arm around her and she nestled against me like some furry animal. Before I knew it she was sitting astride me and the kissing really started. In between we were whispering.

"You're nice."

"You're very nice too."

"I haven't got any knickers on."

If ever there was an invitation this was it. I had my jeans off in seconds and Roz started bouncing around on my dick like a mad puppet. This was all going splendidly when I suddenly noticed the figure of Mike sidling past. He peered myopically in our direction.

"Great party. Enjoying it?"

Fortunately, we had both come to a few conclusions before we started laughing.

By squeezing all my possessions into the car I could move everything to London in one trip. The route would soon become familiar—Chiswick, Hammersmith Bridge—following the curve of the Thames until I came to Fulham Palace Rd. As soon as I could see Imperial College I knew I was nearly home. For the foreseeable future, Barstowe would be just another place I went to visit.

Bronsart Rd. was little different from many of the rows of Victorian terraced houses in West London. The shopkeepers were less friendly, part of that metropolitan indifference to everyone's existence, but I soon got used to that. Strolling in the grounds of Fulham Palace Cemetery—delightfully haphazard and overgrown—became a regular respite from the urban vista.

I always paid the rent on time and having no landlord anywhere near was a bonus. As the summer approached, the garden came into its own and was a glorious haven of an evening.

Naturally, my parents wondered how I was doing but, by making judicious visits at Christmas and Easter, I mostly satisfied my mother's curiosity. Affection for my parents I most certainly owned but, being an only child, it had been necessary early in my life to perfect ways of avoiding too much interrogation.

Kelston Productions shared office space with Sparkes Studios in a building near Blythe House. West Kensington was only a mile away and, after a few weeks I thought about contacting Douglas. I did have mixed feelings about this and concluded he was simply an enigma. His imperious stance was combined with a licence that would have been the envy of any anarchist. This paradox inevitably led to unconsidered decisions and, as had been demonstrated, frequent disasters.

In deciding to seek him out, my real reservation was the possibility of meeting Tommy Box. He was, however, nowhere to be seen when I was eventually reunited with Douglas. Would he still be smarting from the rebellion during the making of *Stilton*? If so, he concealed this most admirably, and was extremely cordial. He even offered me a month's work as AD on a production run by a friend of his. I accepted with alacrity. Douglas was to play a further part in my future though I did not know so at the time.

Wanting to make another movie of my own was an itch that would not go away. I had never written a screenplay before, but a few scripts had been made available in the 1960s and I set about studying these. Quickly learning some of the basic rules—description of place has to be functional, insight into a character's mood or motives rarely stated—I was soon becoming au fait with the form. I also realised that dialogue must either move the narrative along or tell the audience more about the character, nothing else. Interaction between characters holds the audience's attention far more than dramatic action—they can relate to it better. Ultimately movies were about *people*—and made for *other people* to watch. If an audience could not identify with the characters, or feel sympathetic towards them, the movie would fail. All the razzamatazz in the world would not save a naive script.

Writing convincing dialogue is not easy and a technique many novelists never master. What makes dialogue 'work' is not only reproducing inflections of speech, but reproducing how people interact. Conversation is rarely anything but spontaneous and *how* lines are delivered in a movie is all important. Directing actors was going to be a whole new world for me too. Actors act, directors direct. Although that might seem obvious, it was an element in movie making often forgotten. How a director shaped a scene was, I suspected, an art only gained by experience.

I had not contacted Pete since I had moved, but somehow he already knew I was no longer in Barstowe.

"Up there in the smoke now, eh?"

"Listen, I need your advice."

"Oh, yeah? What's that?"

"Approaching Kelston Productions about funding …"

As always, Pete was eager to exchange some level of gossip.

"I heard there was a bit of trouble on that movie you were AD on …"

"Tempers did get a bit frayed."

Pete sounded confidential.

"I don't think the squabbles stopped there either. More rows in post apparently."

"Is *Stilton* going to come out then?"

"No mention in the trades …"

I returned to my original thesis.

"The thing is, I want to get some money out of Douglas …"

"You do?"

"To film a screenplay I'm writing. I want to direct too."

I could almost hear Pete thinking.

"If he puts up the funding … won't Douglas want to run the show? That was why there was all that trouble in Devon wasn't it? Or so Phil Brooks was telling me."

"I know … that is a worry … but I've got to give it a try."

"Why not? If you're still pals with him."

"Seem to be."

"You could look at it this way … if he's had two duds, he might welcome you to find a winner."

"That's a good way of looking at it."

"Save his reputation, kind of …"

The more I thought about it, the more I was somehow convinced Pete was right.

While working on the new Kelston production I got to know a few of the crew members and some of the cast. Martine had caught my eye from the beginning—French, petite and smart. On set, she had great confidence which made her performances sing. We talked together about movies and shared future ambitions. It soon became clear these might be fruitfully combined. We decided to write a screenplay together.

Martine suggested the story should have the *Commedia dell'arte* as its theme. The roles in the story are clear-cut—Pierrot the sad clown, the worldly Harlequin, and Columbine, the woman they both desire. We added another female character—Marie—so as not to be restricted by the eternal triangle. We stuck to the tradition that Pierrot never gets the girl or, in our story, either of them. The power would reside with Harlequin. He was to be cast as an older man and a counterpoint, owning both women—one as his wife, the other as his mistress.

In our minds we were already casting the parts. Martine suggested Nicholas Gilbey to play Harlequin. An Englishman who lived in Paris, where part of the movie would be shot, he was well-liked there. Martine would play the wife and Suzanne—an actress friend of hers in London—the mistress. We decided on a fey American that we had met on the Kelston set for the Pierrot role.

"*C'est parfait*! The Harlequin man is just as my stepfather in Grenoble. I do not think he has a mistress, my mother would not allow such a thing, but he is a boulevardier. *Tiens!* It is just as well my mother is *tres riche* and gives him an allowance!"

We produced a first draft of the screenplay.

SCENE 1 EXT DAY

We see a dark raging sea, close up of waves.
Screen switches to black, white titles.

VOICE

Quel est le sujet du film?
Was ist der Film?
¿cuál es la película?

Screen returns to black, voice continues.

VOICE

When we look at the light we forget what darkness is, but when we are in the dark we imagine that light.

SCENE 2 EXT DAY

A fine day. A young woman with long dark hair is looking out to sea. The sunlight catches her hair and the sea breeze moves the strands of hair. She turns SR and we see her face in profile; she is looking intently into the distance.

VOICE

What do we know about her, what do we need to know?

As an added twist Martine proposed that Marie and Columbine could also be lovers. I must have looked surprised.

"Oui! *Les Lesbienne. C'est l'amour* … in every way … nothing else matters."

Without Martine I would not have been able to write convincingly of love. I admitted to her I did not understand its ways. Martine used the simple ploy of making me fall in love with her, something which was easy to do. She would later take me to the heights of passion and beyond; how two lovers may know an eternal moment together. Martine also taught me the meaning of longing while she was schooling me in the ways of the heart. In matters of love, women are the professionals.

I drew up some storyboards as best I could. Now I knew exactly what shots we needed, and the whole started to take shape as a movie. We worked hard together on the dialogue and the rhythm of the story. After two weeks, apart from a few minor revisions, all was complete and we decided to celebrate.

For a suitable French feast, I bought Brie, pate, a loaf and a good claret. I set everything out neatly on the table and even added a vase of flowers. Martine was delighted.

"Oh, that is so beautiful ... thank you, *mon cher*."

We stood together and she kissed me on the lips. The brief gesture meant much. We might have embraced briefly before, but this was different. Lingering over the next kiss, Martine held both my hands in hers and we looked longingly at each other.

"Now we have finished our work, it is time for us to play."

"That sounds like a good idea."

"I think it is right your star should get to know the director, don't you?"

"Intimately ..."

"*D'accord*, I am yours completely ... I give you *la permission* ... you may know every part of me."

Clothed, Martine was beautiful, naked, even more so. Supper was forgotten for the moment, other appetites needing to be satisfied. Later, as we lay in each other's arms we exchanged caresses and endearments.

"*Mon amour*, are you taking notes?"

"Do you think I should?"

"Non. There are more important things to do right now."

The next moment Martine was astride me, expertly taking me into herself.

"*C'est belle …*"

Night had fallen by the time Martine led me to the supper table.

"It would be so *triste* not to eat this beautiful feast."

We were merry and light when we went back to bed.

"Now you must love me like only a real man may do."

"Didn't I do that before?"

"*Vraiment*, but now I wish you to do that to me even more so."

I obliged, and Martine fell asleep with a smile on her lips. I gazed upon the woman who was without doubt my first real love.

Douglas was, as ever, faultlessly polite when I called him.

"I wondered if I could come over and run a couple of ideas past you …"

"Sure, sure. Do that, anytime."

"Are you around tomorrow?"

"Yeah, come over in the morning."

I paused for maximum effect.

"I'll be bringing my friend Martine ... you'll like her ..."

The tone changed ever so slightly, the bait taken.

"Fine, see you then."

I phoned Martine straightaway; she sounded more than excited.

"*Alors!* So this might just be happening, eh?"

"Nothing sorted yet, we've just got to go and talk to Douglas about it all ..."

Martine paused.

"*L'aristocrate tres riche, non?* Shall I dress sexy for milord?"

"You always do ..."

"I can be even more so ... believe me ... there is no limit ..."

"Sounds great. I'll like it anyway ..."

"I know that, you naughty boy."

When they met, Douglas was certainly taken with Martine. If she had sat in his lap, he would probably have agreed to any proposal we might have offered. After some preliminary spiel I passed over a budget I had prepared. Douglas donned his glasses and examined this carefully, or appeared to. He sat back and regarded us, or mostly Martine.

"Thirty thousand, yeah?"

"We can bring it in for that if we stick to a skeleton crew and a small cast ..."

"You've got a finished screenplay?"

"Right here."

I passed this over.

"*La Mer, la Belle Mer....*"

Martine leaned forward just enough to display a little more of her charms. She spoke softly, as if Douglas was the only man in the entire world.

"We would like to film in Paris ... in the Spring. *D'accord.*"

Martine could always hint at anything with every word she said. She casually licked her lips.

"It would be so lovely to do that."

If this performance didn't do the trick nothing would, I thought. Douglas, who had been studying a few pages of the screenplay, put this aside.

"Okay, I'll see if it's the kind of project Kelston would like to be involved with ... if it is, then I can see about raising some investment."

Martine bounded into the air and clapped her hands, a performance which obviously entranced Douglas

"*Merveilleux!* Oh, that's wonderful. So exciting."

Douglas turned to me.

"I've got a co-producer in mind if we do go ahead ... Kenny Rolands ... we can work together."

This shone a warning light, but I said nothing.

"We'll speak to you soon, Douglas."

"Sure."

As we left Martine embraced Douglas, a gesture he had hopefully been anticipating.

"Thank you so very much."

We made our way into Kensington in search of a cab. I was already planning my next move, to speak to Kenny, the producer who had been mentioned. This was crucial. If Douglas behaved as he had on the *Stilton* set we were doomed before we began.

* * *

Getting Kenny's phone number from Pete required some subterfuge on my part. Thankfully he did not quiz me too much. Confiding in one person might be okay, sharing a secret with a third party is always dangerous. Later, I called Kenny and introduced myself.

"Hi, I'm Jack Strange …"

"You're the guy making the French film …"

"You knew?"

"Sure. There's me, and Douglas producing."

I detected Kenny was not keen on the arrangement.

"That's what I wanted to talk to you about."

"Go ahead, I'm listening."

"I've worked with Douglas a couple of times … on the second movie there were problems …"

Kenny was quickly onto this.

"He did tell me … in his own roundabout way."

"I don't want that to happen again … with *my* movie."

"No, I can see you wouldn't."

Kenny was good with the pregnant pauses, almost as expert as a midwife.

"Why don't you just have me producing?"

"Exactly what I was thinking."

"It *sounds* okay. I can only ask Douglas and see what he says."

"Be great if you could sort that out … and there is one other thing …"

"What's that?"

"The cameraman … I want to use Phil Brooks."

"Yeah, I know Phil … he's really good."

"The problem is … on the set of *Stilton* … he and Douglas had words …"

"So, you don't want Douglas to know you're using Phil …"

"Exactly. I haven't told Phil that Douglas and Kelston might be funding us either."

"They *could* both find out, but I'd be there to smooth things out if that actually happened."

I breathed again.

"Thanks."

"Frankly, I think Douglas has forgotten all about what happened back then anyway."

"He certainly hasn't mentioned it when I've seen him."

I refrained from enquiring what happened with the *Stilton* movie. Pete had probably told me all there was to know anyway.

"So, is there anything else you need? Anything your producer can provide, Mr. Director?"

I tried to be serious, now conscious of my new status.

"I'd like to check something with Martine … she's my leading actress … around costumes, maybe props too?"

"She's French?"

"Right. If you two could have a word together about all that …"

"Fine with me."

After talking to Kenny, I felt much easier. Over the years, whenever our paths crossed, she would always have that effect on me.

* * *

An anxious week followed, but when Douglas contacted me, all sounded, promising.

"Kelston certainly wants to be involved … and we've managed to secure twenty-five thousand."

I nearly let out a whoop of excitement.

"That's fantastic, but I do have a feeling we're going to need the other five …"

"I agree. Looking at the script that buffer ought to be there … especially if you're filming abroad."

"I don't plan on that bit being too extravagant. Martine has a few contacts in Paris, obviously."

Douglas was all efficiency.

"I'd suggest you try to get a grant for the rest. Kenny can help you with all that. I'll get her to give you a call."

"Great. Thanks."

I called Martine to tell her the news but she wasn't there. A few minutes later Kenny rang.

"Hey, this is all good, yeah?"

"Absolutely. There is the business with the grant though …"

"For the other five grand?"

"Can you help me with …"

"Approaching people and writing applications? I'm sure I can …"

We talked about the cast. Martine had already confirmed that everyone was available and I gave Kenny their contact details. We agreed that we would all meet at my flat the next day. When the two women met there was a hint of two cats circling each other. I was not to discover what was behind that little episode until many years later. Kenny was open about the role of Douglas in the coming production.

"The funds are coming from some business consortium he's been liaising with, so he's agreed to be EP. There's no reason for him to have any direct input in the filming."

"Right."

Kenny must have noted my look of relief.

"If the sponsors have any questions about anything then he'll put them straight on to me. I can't see that happening, the deal is all pretty straight forward, as deals go."

She produced some forms from her case.

"We've got to get this grant application in straight away. It's all here, mostly stuff about budgets and projected gross ... that kind of thing."

We sat at the table and toiled away together at this while, at the same time, Martine showed Kenny some sketches she had made for costumes. I was impressed that Kenny could focus on both tasks at once. When the grant application was eventually finished and signed, Kenny slid the papers back into her bag.

"The best bet we have with all this is Douglas' name as a guarantor. His family is big pals with Lord somebody or other who's on the board."

"How long will it be before they let us know?"

"Two or three weeks ... depends on how many other applications they've got to go through at the moment."

After Kenny left, Martine and I went to bed together.

"That girl. Do you think she is attractive?"

I was softly stroking her when she said this.

"Not as much as you."

"*Stupide!* I was not asking that."

I halted in mid-caress.

"She's okay."

"*D'accord.* You don't fancy her. That's good enough."

I resumed my attentions and Martine responded with her usual enthusiasm.

As Kenny had predicted, Douglas' name did give weight to our application. Two weeks later I received a cheque for £5,000 from the Arts organisation we had approached. Now we were ready to roll. On the Friday before we started shooting the crew gathered at the location, a house at the Islington end of Camden Town. This belonged to a friend of Douglas who had just sold his flat in Chelsea. He would not be moving in for at least a week; the empty property was perfect for my purposes.

I had brought fold-up chairs and a camping table with me, adequate enough for our initial meeting. Kenny provided the makings of coffee, and as soon as everyone arrived we got down to business. Being reunited with Phil and Steve felt good, and they had brought Crystal, the make–up artist from Devon, who I also liked. Kenny had organised a lighting crew and Jeff had called, agreeing to edit the film. All seemed to bode well.

The filming would be split between London and Paris, the restraints of the budget obliging us to take as few people as possible to France. Kenny was already nervous about our expenses in Paris. I took the view that our arrangements there would look after themselves. Instinctively, I believed that Martine would, on her own territory, take charge.

Getting to know our Islington location, even for a few hours after the meeting, was a bonus for me. I was able to gauge just how much light came into each room at any particular time of the day. I didn't expect to be able to give the same attention to the interiors in France, as we would not have the luxury of so much time for the set-ups.

8

My debut as a director on my first film was not quite how I had imagined it would be. While rehearsing Suzanne in the first scene, she finished her line and gestured to me. I came nearer and she began to whisper.

"I don't want anybody to know this. I've never acted in front of a camera before."

"Oh …"

"We did a bit of photography stuff in drama school, but never anything serious like this. I should have said before …"

I was determined to handle my first challenge as a director with aplomb.

"Just relax, make sure you know the lines with Martine. I'll maybe suggest things as we go along."

Suzanne put her hand on mine.

"Alright. Thanks."

She smiled up at me, somewhat invitingly I thought. Martine who had been watching all this must have picked up on the vibes too. She walked over, put her arm through mine and led me away

"We must start work now, *M'sieu Le Cinéaste.*"

We had at least five set-ups to get through, and Suzanne was in half of them. If she needed constant guidance, time was going to be tight.

"As soon as Phil decides where he wants the lights we're away. Can you and Suzanne do one more run through from where you come in?"

"Okay."

Thus began the first day. We got through all the scenes I wanted. Phil and I experimented with lenses and angles, and I was happy with everything. If this was what film-making was all about, I knew I was going to like it.

The lighting crew turned out to be on the money and fitted in perfectly with the rest of the crew. Like all good crew, they knew what was essential and what was possible. They asked me what look I wanted and, every time, they delivered. To satisfy myself, I wanted to go through some of the repertoire of lighting effects—what corresponded with heightened emotion, power and suspense. To me, these were the key elements of drama. Just through the colour and texture of a scene—hard and soft light came into this—I wanted to tangibly convey atmosphere. Although the theme of the movie was light and romantic, I didn't want to drift into vague whimsy. Dark and light, gritty and chic I wanted it all in there.

Setting up a shot in a movie is very like writing a scene in a novel. There are unlimited possibilities in the way it may be depicted. What is significant, however, is the manner in which the author, or the director, wants his audience to interpret what they are experiencing. Of course, every individual perceives things in a different way, but in this aspect of the process, the artist is God. The advantage to me of working with such a professional crew was that I could suggest how I saw the scene being shot and they would endeavour to manifest my vision. Phil was never shy about telling us how we could enhance a particular effect, and for that alone he was worth his (considerable) weight in gold. My vocabulary of shots too was increasing daily and, by the time we got to France, I was flying high.

I had planned for plenty of guerrilla filming in Paris since the chance of us falling foul of the Parisian authorities was always possible, if not extremely likely. Being chased along the *Rue Saint Honore* at midnight by a posse of gendarmes was the most dramatic episode, playing hide and seek in the *le Jardin des Tuileries* another. During all these adventures Phil was as crazy and determined as we were. I was in great spirits, excited to be in Paris, and particularly in the company of Martine whose home it was.

We shot some gorgeous dawn footage in the Pere Lachaise cemetery and some hand-held stuff in the Metro and on the boulevards. For a heavy man, Phil could balance his own body weight superbly and achieve a smooth pan. Sometimes he shot from a low angle, or used a wide lens to eliminate any chance of jerkiness. Memories of seeing *The Red Balloon* as a child made me seek out some of the locations in the district of *Belleville*. It was a disappointment, nearly all was gone, only a little of the magic remaining, the rest a graffiti covered hell.

We filmed our interiors in Montmartre where

Martine had friends. Here, I did have the chance to work with colour, as the apartment was filled with Moroccan hangings, Moorish furniture and screens. I employed as subtle a palette as I could, one away from primary colours so as to resemble classical paintings. From the warm shadows of Rembrandt to the dramatic forms in Caravaggio, every gradation of tone was important.

Besides using Autumn colours for evening interiors and bright broken light in the mornings, I wanted to break a few rules too. Could I make blue advance and orange recede? Simple conventions like having a character in light clothes against a dark background I wanted to ignore, at least momentarily. In the climax to the story the audience must decide for themselves whether Marie has been deceiving them or not. By shooting Suzanne at eye level and talking to camera we achieved this. None of the other characters have a soliloquy, so the clue is always there for an audience to detect.

Our other problem was how to depict the death of the Harlequin character. The notion of a well-deserved fate for the villain was far too clichéd. By making his demise almost surreal, using the equivalent of a transparent screen—in practice the thinnest shower curtain we could find—we got the effect I wanted.

Away from these aesthetic triumphs, we had not been so lucky with the company who hired the lights. They were surly and inefficient, and I was at a big disadvantage not speaking the language. When Martine decided to get involved it all changed. If the pompous Algerian boss thought he was going to get the better of her, he was mistaken. For every Gallic curse he mouthed at her, Martine gave back as good as she got and soon emerged the victor. I thought I would have to step in at one point and so did Phil, but it was all pure theatre. This game of threat and counter-threat is played out every day by the inhabitants of every city in Europe.

Kenny had decided that her presence in Paris was an unnecessary expense, and that daily phone calls to London would be adequate to keep up with the action. Back in England, we were reunited at Leighton House, where we had arranged to film for two days. We had little time for small talk. To hire the venue had been costly, but ultimately it was worth it. The location would double as Marrakesh, the rendezvous of Pierrot and Marie.

The richness of the Moorish decoration in the Arab Hall proved to be almost overwhelming, but by using screens and gauze we tempered the luminosity a little. A fountain was the centrepiece of the main gallery and, by varying the depth of field and carefully using filters, we achieved some remarkable effects. Experimenting with different backgrounds for close-ups, combined with Suzanne's extensive wardrobe, gave us endless possibilities in colour and pattern.

Phil almost doubled as AD. If I missed an angle or a covering shot he would quietly mention it and away we went again. He was always on the lookout for cutaways too, his favourite remark being, 'Got to keep the editor happy'. After a wrap-party even more modest than that held in Devon, we handed the footage into Jeff's waiting hands.

I called Kenny after a few weeks to check on progress.

"How's it looking do you think?"

She sounded cautious but optimistic.

"Okay when I saw a rough cut of the fine cut."

"How's the sound d'you think? I was a bit worried about some of those rooms being a bit echoey."

"In Leighton House? I really thought that was going to be terrible too, but its fine."

I reprised.

"So ... audio post and music still to do, yeah? What's the music going to be d'you reckon?"

"Classical ... no rights to pay."

I put in a little tease.

"We could have used really corny accordion music for the Paris bits ..."

"Definitely not!"

"Steve has some tapes of this way-out surf band he recorded in Long Beach. Jeff tried synching it with some of the Metro footage and it works incredibly well."

"Now, don't get too way out ..."

"Don't worry it won't end up as pretentious tosh, I'll make sure of that."

Kenny sounded relieved.

By Douglas pulling all the right strings, *La Mer* was shown at the BFI London Film festival. If the movie didn't quite get a standing ovation, it achieved the nearest thing to it. We were in with even more of a chance when *La Mer* got a complimentary review in one of the posh papers. The title of the article was—*A Different French Connection.*

'La Mer, la Belle Mer'. (1974)

Jane Birkin's piece of aural soft porn 'Je t'aime' is still fresh enough in the public mind to associate all things French with the promise of a generous serving of sauce. If it is the sensual you are looking for in a movie you cannot go far wrong with 'La Mer, la Belle Mer'. (dir. Jack Strange). As Jean-Luc Godard cast Brigitte Bardot in 'Le Mepris', the lead actress Martine Gidot is worthy of the role of siren. The punters will be delighted by a glance at a boob or two, not to mention a sinuous thigh. That she is in bed with another woman at the same time simply adds to the spice.

Filmed both in London and Paris, it is to the credit of the filmmakers how seamless is the transition from one location to another. The classical, smoky English cityscape harmonises lyrically with the chic beauty of urban France

Superb support from Suzanne Forest and Danny Burns enhances Martine's pouting performance. Nicholas Gilbey triumphs as the roué, venal but always evoking our sympathy. We are almost willing that he will, in the end, be forgiven

An accolade must be given for the camerawork, excelling throughout, and the soundtrack is original and compelling. The editing is snappy, original and unfailingly reflects the varying pace. The attention never wanders while watching 'La Mer, la Belle Mer'.

Jack Strange, veteran of shorts and documentary work but new to features, has not disappointed with this, his first offering. The debut is not only polished and slick but innovative, probably revolutionary. We shall hear more from this talented auteur whose work is skilful enough to stand with any first division director working today.

With Kenny's help and a nudge from Douglas we submitted *La Mer* to all the major European Film Festivals of 1975. I would have liked to travel to Europe to follow the movie's progress but this would not have been prudent. After settling my rent and a few bills with my meagre director's fee, I was barely solvent. I found out later that the movie had been screened at a premium time and in the best venue at Cannes. One of the judges had been a big fan of *Good Scene*, my Sixties movie shown in San Francisco. Upon such apparent coincidences does our destiny depend.

The phone summoned me a few nights later. I hardly recognized Pete's voice.

"You've won the fucking *Palme D'Or* ..."

"*What?*"

"Yeah, really ... it was on the telly ... report from Cannes."

"Amazing. I didn't think we had a hope in hell."

"What other festivals did you put in for?"

"Berlin, Venice ..."

"European tour for you then, mate. You lucky dog."

I kept *stumm*, not so much at being embarrassed by my personal circumstances, but because I was stunned at the news. I put the phone down and it rang again immediately; this time it was Kenny calling from the Film Festival. She sounded more than slightly drunk and most of what she said made little sense. She was also trying to make herself heard over an oompah band playing in the background and the prolonged yells of revellers. Martine was next to call.

"It is so wonderful. I am so happy for us. I come to you now and we will make love *beaucoup de fois* to celebrate."

That prospect was worth more than a dozen prizes, even the Palme D'or. A bird in the hand, and all that. Later, in bed Martine confided in me.

"Douglas was there at the festival with Kenny, you could see them together on the TV. Our milord he is having an affair with her *je suis certaine*."

"Quite probably. He has a certain reputation for …"

"I know. Some of the girls on the set when we met … they warn me about him."

"When you met him he must have known you were with me. …"

"*Oui, je sais*. He still phone me."

"Really?"

"I do not how he got the number. I had never spoken to him before we went to the office."

"Cheeky sod!"

"Yes, he wanted us to meet somewhere, and when

I said it was *impossible* he did not understand. I think all these girls just say yes to him all the time, *sans une pensee*."

I turned over to look at Martine.

"I always want you to say yes to me."

"I do, my beautiful man, because I want to feel you inside me *tous les fois*."

Within moments I made that happen.

Communication wasn't quite so all-embracing or instant, forty years ago. Pete was my main informant on the progress of *La Mer*.

"You got the *Silver Bear* at Berlin as well but I'm glad to say you were only *nominated* for *The Golden Lion* in Venice, or your head would be so big you wouldn't be able to get out the door."

"That's utterly amazing."

"So how does it feel, Jack being a cult figure ... one so young?"

I laughed at the time, I could do nothing else. Decades later, *La Mer* joined a list of late-night, must-see cult films; I never dreamed of that happening.

From the less than friendly place it had first appeared to be, London now began to feel like home for me. The movie biz was definitely a small world and I saw familiar faces all the time. Things changed too when *La Mer* got the recognition it did. I was about to move up to the next rung of the ladder.

I didn't see Douglas until negotiations for a distribution deal were happening. Kenny was in charge of all this, helped by Matt Dundon, at one time Kenny's boyfriend. A Rottweiler of a guy, he had no illusions about the ways of film distributors and had his own methods of dealing with them.

"We've got to hire screening time somewhere so these blokes will come and have a look. You've gotta get all of 'em at once … that's the hard bit. Winning prizes at festivals might give you some clout, but it don't guarantee nothing."

I was apprehensive.

"That's going to cost …"

Kenny stepped in.

"Doug will put the money up I'm sure."

Matt continued.

"It's the only way ahead. You can't contact 'em … those geezers one a time. What happens if someone says it's no good? Word gets out … you're in shit street. I'm tellin' you, mate, these are hard bastards. But you still gotta get 'em on your side."

Douglas did sort out a deal, one which returned the funding to the investor and also provided an amount for our publicity. We got distribution and *La Mer* went into profit straightaway when it was released—usually as half of an art movie programme. At least it got shown on the regular cinema circuit and I was more than happy with that. I didn't want it to get lost with the more obscure film club stuff, worthy maybe, but not commercial.

Douglas had enthusiastically joined in with the razzmatazz when *La Mer* was on a roll with the festival awards. He had obviously enjoyed sharing the limelight with Kenny. Away from the stage, he was to be seen surrounded constantly by a horde of starlets and their ilk. Years later I thought about his role in the world of movies and how very few, apart from his temporary female admirers, wholly accepted him.

Hollywood, in line with the American Dream, embraces the man who has risen from humble beginnings and becomes Head of Studio. Wardour Street was more capricious with its accolades, longevity being the quality deemed most deserving of any reward. Unfortunately for him, Viscount Hampton did not fit into either camp.

A month later Martine returned to Paris, this time for good. Although I had always known it was inevitable—her French fiancée being mentioned once in a while during our liaison—I had tried to ignore this.

I was unaware that while we were filming in Paris, Martine was studiously avoiding any parts of the city where he might be. Interest in *La Mer* inevitably faded and I never saw her again. Only once, in a TV documentary twenty years later recalling indie movies of the Seventies, I caught Martine on screen talking about *La Mer*.

In the next few years, lucky breaks had a habit of evading me and there were times when I only just managed to stay afloat in London. Projects were always on the brink of happening before falling at the last hurdle. The notion of filming someone else's script had never occurred to me; I was convinced I was exclusively of the auteur breed. At the beginning of 1978 a novel—*Such Stuff* by Gavin Munford— came unexpectedly into my orbit.

After university I had read little, post-modern novels particularly passing me by. On one of the rare occasions when I did browse among the bookshops on the Charing Cross Road, I came across a stack of Munford's novel. This, the current offering, had been more than a moderate success. I picked up a copy and began leafing through it. Hardly had I started doing this when an assistant rushed up to me.

"If you would like, we can provide you with a signed copy. Gavin Munford … the author … is here doing a signing today. Would you like to meet him?"

I was easy about the offer.

"Yeah, okay."

After following the assistant to another part of the store, I saw Munford ensconced at a table with yet another pile of his works. He rose to greet me, a bearded, friendly cove in corduroys.

"Hello, hello."

Noticing me rather diffidently clutching his novel he laughed.

"You don't *have* to buy it you know …"

"I probably will."

"Good man. Who shall I sign it to?"

"Jack Strange."

Munford opened the book at the flyleaf and paused.

"I know that name. Aren't you a film director?"

"I like to think so."

"You made that amazing French film … set in Paris …"

I agreed, depreciatingly.

"*La Mer, la Belle Mer.*"

"Hey, great meeting you …"

Munford waved his pen around.

"You're exactly the guy we need …"

"I am?"

"Friend of mine wants to put the dosh up to film this very book of mine …"

While we were talking a queue of punters had appeared behind me, Munford scribbled a number on the back of his card.

"Give this guy … Charles Fry his name is … a call."

Munford also scrawled his signature inside the book and handed it to me. He was laughing.

"You don't have to pay for it."

Thanking him, I left the shop. I could still hear his laughter when I was in the street.

* * *

Charles Fry was the same vintage as Munford, but decidedly more smooth. No corduroys for him—expensive tailoring, on the flash side. We met in the garden of a pub in Hammersmith.

"So you're the famous director, eh?"

"Not that famous."

"Good enough for us, I'm sure."

Charles was rapidly losing his hair making him look a lot older than he probably was. He took a sip of ale.

"I ought to explain, all this is the fault of my accountant. He's decided the best way to clear up all the odds and sods of business I've been involved with over the past five years …"

I waited.

"… is to start a new company."

I nodded, assuming this was probably the sort of thing accountants tell rich people.

"A movie production company by any chance?"

"I registered it a couple of weeks ago. *Movie Mister* I decided to call it. I'm going to be Mr. Movies, eh?"

I didn't feel like ladling out any encouragement.

"If you're *very* lucky."

Charles wasn't fazed.

"I'm glad you said that, shows you've got your head screwed on, but I'm willing to take a punt. It either goes to the tax man, or pays someone's bills … yours probably."

The baited hook, one I wasn't going to take quite that easily.

"But why get involved in *movies*? There must be plenty of other things to invest in, things you probably ..."

"... know a lot more about? Dozens, but I'm really doing old Gavin a favour ... get his name in lights. I've known him for a long time ... he's actually a jolly good writer."

"I have read the book. It certainly keeps you interested."

"I think it'll make a bloody good film."

"That's up to who directs it ... and the actors ... simple really."

"I agree ... that's why we're talking now."

I eyed him quizzically.

"Is there a screenplay?"

"Yes ... or at least there will be very soon. We've commissioned a good bloke to write it."

"Right."

Charles looked me over.

"You might think it's a strange title, but Gavin and I thought we'd go with the book ..."

"Shakespeare ... 'such stuff as dreams are made on'. It's a pretty well known quote."

Charles nodded briefly, as if he was not particular interested in the Bard or literature either.

"Who's going to produce?"

"*I am.*"

I looked across the table.

"*And* you're putting up the investment?"

Charles took a swig of beer, almost defiantly.

"Right. Is that unusual?"

"To be EP and producer? It's not unknown ..."

He interrupted.

"But ..."

"Possible conflict of interest ..."

He regarded me carefully.

"Interfering in what goes on ... how things are done?"

I was determined not to mention the Devon fiasco.

"Rows between directors and studios about budgets are quite legendary."

"I suppose that's understandable ... on both sides."

"Possibly, though I don't suppose a plumber likes to have the householder telling him how to fit a tap."

"If *you* were the director on this, let's say, you wouldn't appreciate anyone poking their nose in all the time."

I deflected the question as best I could.

"You need someone to do the day to day organising ... a *line producer* is the usual go-between."

"Trouble shooter?"

"Sort of ... taking care of any hassles that might come up, really. Going to meetings, liaising ... everything that needs doing away from the actual movie."

"If you were involved, could you find someone like that?"

"I might be able to. The point is that's only *one* of the crew ..."

"Could we leave all that in your hands, though?"

I stared at him, even though I was trying not to.

"Getting the crew together?"

I pondered. At least I would have people I knew around me, if I was to agree to be involved, that was.

"I suppose so …"

Charles raised a finger skyward, like a Roman emperor.

"As for the cast … actors I can provide … more than enough."

I realised that nothing I had experienced in movies so far had prepared me for a set-up like this.

"I've got several interests in drama schools … in fact I own one."

My eyes went out over the Thames, wondering what this particular stretch of the river had seen over the centuries. The thought kept the present in perspective.

"Do you have an actual budget in mind?"

At the mention of money Charles features became illuminated.

"What do you think? Three?

"Three million?

"Not enough?"

"Well, I haven't seen the screenplay yet, but unless you want thousands of extras … like *Lawrence of Arabia* … I think that should let us in with a chance."

"Good. I'm pretty sure it's all set in England, no *foreign* locations."

He said the word with slight distaste.

"I have access to so some nice places here … country houses … stately homes. I know quite a few nobs."

For one terrible moment I thought Charles might mention Douglas and the family seat—Mahogany

House—but it was not to be.

"There's quite a bit of that sort of thing in the book … hunt balls … shootin' and fishin'."

"It's the American market we're after … they love all that sort of guff."

Charles gave me the piercing look, doubtless part of his armoury.

"So you fancy coming in with us?"

"I don't see why not … the sooner you get the screenplay done though, the better."

"I'll give the scribe a rocket, tell him we want it pronto."

"And when do you want to start shooting?"

"Anytime you like old boy. You're in the driving seat now."

It was all very well to say that, but what would we find at the end of the trip?

The screenplay arrived by courier two days later, along with a contract. I gave both items the once over. I was pleasantly surprised to find the screenplay was a competent effort, certainly filmable. A love story with a modicum of drama—not enough to make it a thriller—its own particular charm made the story work. The screenwriter had sharpened up the action in the original so the exposition was totally clear.

Before I finally committed myself, I would consult the oracle. As soon as I got Pete on the line he made me feel better. I sometimes wondered if he was the older brother I never had.

"About time you had a break, all that talent … masterpieces of cinema begging to be created."

"Yeah, yeah. But what do you think?"

"It does all sound like a vanity project, but if the money's there, so what?"

"This Charles bloke told me it was all a tax shelter, or something, for his company."

"So he doesn't care whether it's a flop or not?"

Once more I thought of Douglas and his ill-fated adventures.

"Maybe not. I never know where blokes like that are coming from."

Pete had no time for the mysterious.

"How's the budget?"

"Three."

"Better if it was ten, you could get some names in there and go to town."

"You really think that's necessary? The script's good."

Pete took a breath.

"I hate to undermine your high artistic ideals, Jack, but I don't actually think the storyline makes much odds these days."

"No?"

"That's just the way it is I'm sure. The movie-going public are now totally star-struck. We're going to see bigger and bigger budgets because the celebrities will want more and more money, not because the movies themselves are necessarily going to be any better."

"Doesn't sound too good."

"It's not … the beginning of the end where serious, thoughtful movies are concerned. It's going to be all popcorn and candy floss from now on, I'm telling you."

Another thoughtful pause.

"Who will do distribution on your little epic?"

"America apparently. Fifties costume drama … post-war England … all supposed to go down well over there."

Pete didn't sound convinced.

"Maybe. That market is so fickle though … even the BBC stuff isn't guaranteed to catch every time these days."

"Charles seems to be a global wheeler dealer …"

Pete was brisk.

"So he may be, but if there's no names, and not much of a hook then he probably won't get much of a deal. That's the other thing … marketing. That's where the money's all going to go soon too."

I tried to be positive, not an altogether easy task.

"I get to choose the crew … *he's* providing the cast."

Pete exploded.

"Ha! A mixed bag of luvvies!"

"Will it be like that?"

"If it is, I don't envy you directing a bunch of D list actors. Don't say I didn't warn you."

With Pete's words still in my head I still decided to give it a go, and called Charles to tell him so. The contract was the usual standard stuff and I certainly couldn't complain about my director's fee.

Being the pilot didn't stop me feeling lonely on the flight deck. What I needed was some familiar faces around me. I lost no time in contacting Phil and he agreed to work on *Stuff* straight away, along with most of the old firm, as I had come to think of them. I still needed a line-producer, preferably a no-nonsense character, to keep Charles in order.

The next evening Phil and I were ensconced in *The British Bulldog*, a pub in Fulham. Thankfully we had chosen a night when there wasn't a band playing or it would have been impossible to hear a word we said to each other. I got a pint of Fullers in for Phil and a bottled lager for myself. Together we toasted the success of the project, unpredictable though it might be.

"So, what sort of set-up is this? From what you were saying on the blower, not studio finance?"

"Phil, the money's all there … all the rest is up to us."

My man didn't seem too fazed by this.

"Like that is it?"

I nodded.

"What d'you think?"

I waited.

"Could be fine … might even have a laugh … that'd make a change."

"It's filming another book, but this time at least we've got a decent script … budget's good."

Phil shrugged.

"The money doesn't make a lot of difference, really. You still got to point the camera at something, or someone, and film it. It's getting it all done is the thing that's important."

I reflected.

"From my point of view, this is a step-up from our little adventure in France."

"Don't knock it! You did okay on that. Christ! You won all them prizes."

"You wouldn't think so though. This is the first thing I've been offered since then."

Phil sat back.

"Feast or famine, that's the way of it. They'll all be after you soon enough, don't you worry."

I readied myself for laying a few cards tablewards.

"Apart from you and the gang, we still need the rest of the crew."

Phil stared a bit at hearing this.

"Haven't you got *anyone* else yet?"

"Charles is the producer and EP."

Phil gave me a searching look.

"Yeah? Does he know anything about making movies?"

I was straight.

"I don't think so … I told him we have to have a line-producer. We need somebody really up together too."

Phil thought hard.

"No worries. I *can* get a good bloke for that … Stuart Warren. He's exactly the opposite of that Tommy idiot. This bloke really knows what he's doing … worked on some big stuff a few years back."

"We need an AD …"

"Yeah, I got someone in mind for that too. Didier … he's French and gay. But he's sound."

I did a mental check-list.

"We do need a locations manager as well … even though Charles has access to all these posh houses in the country, or so he says. Some of the other scenes are right away from all that sort of stuff."

Phil sighed.

"Bit out of my territory, locations manager, but I'm sure it can be done. I'll ask around. You'll want a production manager and designer won't you, if it's costume?"

"Have to. But we can't go too crazy … not too many *assistants* for them."

Phil sighed audibly.

"If it's a *Fifties* thing you're going to want a lot of props … big and little … and cars … all that crap."

"I know. It's when three mil. starts to sound not quite so much after all …"

"That what you got?"

"Yep."

"Well, we can only do what we can do."

Phil leaned over the table.

"D'you want to let me have a copy of the script?"

I handed over the photocopy I'd had printed up for him.

"Great."

Phil finished his drink and stood up—a man with a purpose.

"Right. Better get this sorted …"

"Thanks, Phil, I certainly do appreciate it."

"No worries, mate, we'll get there."

True to his word, Phil had the crew all in place two weeks before the shoot. We had a meeting and arranged all the important stuff. My first sight of the cast, sent along by Charles to a rehearsal studio in Shepherds Bush, was very different. They were being marshalled by Didier and Stuart when I arrived. My new AD was as camp as a row of tents but, beneath the rouge, I detected a shrewd mind. The girls in the cast loved him. Stuart, our resolute LP, was squarish and bald. They made a diverting combination.

Of the actors, some were fresh out of drama school, others were on the fringes of the biz and the rest were posh types taking a chance. I saw a familiar face among the ranks—Martin—who offered a discreet wave. My task was to quickly sort out who could do what, and how well. Didier was succinct from the beginning.

"Philip told me about all this. You have no stars in there, and not much experience either I think?"

"Absolutely right."

Didier looked thoughtful, as well he might.

"It is not like dealing with the pros … then you need the lightest touch, so that they may blossom."

I concurred. Movie acting is a refined skill and the gap between the old-hand and the beginner is as wide as the Grand Canyon.

"It's all very weird … just to be given a whole bunch of actors and not know the first thing about any of them. Like casting in reverse."

"*Exactement*. And even when you find who is suitable you will still need to rehearse all of them … *et beaucoup.*"

"*C'est vrai.*"

Didier smiled

"*Vous parlez Francais, mon ami?*"

"*D'accord … comme un Francais.*"

"*Mon Dieu!* Perhaps you should direct in French"

"It might be more poetic."

He laughed.

"Would you like to know what I think?"

"I was just going to ask you."

Didier beamed.

"We work together today to organise these attractive, but inexperienced people. There will be those who are *impossible* … to them we say *au revoir* … then those who are okay … *peut-etre … et enfin … les acteurs.*"

"Out of those, can we decide who can play the major parts … pretty quickly?"

Didier considered.

"My friend is a drama coach, he would help me. We will choose who we think is good for the part, and either you approve, or you do not."

"Put him on the payroll."

Didier regarded me.

"My friend will come for nothing."

"He will?"

Didier winked.

"He will do it for love."

"Must be a very good friend."

Didier beamed once more.

"Stuart has the first location ready to go …"

I consulted the mental files.

"That the one out of town … in Windsor? I'm sure he emailed me about that this morning, but I was in a rush to get here."

"We start with one of the more simple scenes. The grand pieces are at the Wheatley Estate in Week 2."

On the ball I would have to be.

* * *

Among the potential cast we discovered a thin but rich seam—even a few gems. When I began blocking the first scenes on Day 1, I was far from despondent. While lighting went to work, I discussed the look of the set with Didier, how we could best make use of the space we had been given. A sitting room with French windows that gave access to the garden evoked a solid bourgeois ambiance, perfect for the shot. By shooting tightly in the room and tracking with the characters as they went outside, we could hint at the idea of escape. That had been one of the themes in the book, that of fleeing from stifling convention.

Rehearsals went smoothly enough. I wanted the ambiance to be lively whenever we had any opportunity, to contrast with the implied stiffness of the Fifties. I had already talked briefly to the actors about post-war Britain as I remembered it, something which amused them. What was essential was for them to play in character, not caricature. At first I would insist we stuck rigidly to the lines, any loosening up could come later. Technique definitely needed sharpening up—projecting a mood onto another character, holding the eyes. We got through the first set ups. Day One was in the can!

On Friday afternoon Didier and I sat in my car and talked about how things had been going.

"As long as we can keep going at this pace, I'm happy."

"A happy director … that is what we want."

I smiled briefly.

"Stuart's a good bloke, isn't he?"

"*Oui, tres bon.*"

"So, Monday … everyone has got to get out to Wheatley … over near Uxbridge. It's not all that far. Stuart told me he's got everything organised."

"Have you seen the place yet?"

"I'm going to pop over on the weekend. Have you got any time free?"

"*Oui*, I have … on Sunday."

"If I pick you up in the morning we can have a look at it together. Is that okay?"

"*Parfait.*"

"Stuart has been on his own down there, getting it all sorted out which is too much for anyone. I've said he could have a couple of assistants … and he probably ought to have them on a permanent basis."

"I think you are right. We are back in town for Week 3, yes?"

"Right. Lots of exteriors in Hoxton, or Hackney it might be. Definitely the East End anyway."

Didier looked at me questioningly.

"How many weeks for the whole shoot have we got, Jack?"

"Eight, but I'd like to be ahead of the game after six."

Didier breathed out in Gallic fashion.

"That's very tight."

"I know, but you saw the figures Stuart came up with. We're laying out a fortune on hiring all those props … a third of the budget has gone on costumes and all that already."

"Yes, and I'm sure he's doing deals if he can, asking for favours, collecting them."

"Even so, the big problem is, these props people can charge what they like."

Business over, Didier got out of the car and walked towards where his own vehicle was parked. I could see Martin on the other side of the car park. He waved, and I called out as he started towards me.

"Hi, how's it going? Happy?"

Martin was grinning like a goose.

"Yeah, lots of fun. It's great to see you again, even better you're directing."

"Thank you. It's good to see you too."

In the years since I had seen him, Martin had gained some muscle and a lot of presence.

"Hey, you remember Roz?"

I was wary.

"Mmm."

"She kept asking about you, man. I think you made a bit of a hit there."

I did the cool bit, not very successfully. Gossip on a set was as essential as air, but I didn't need to introduce any more areas of high pressure.

For some reason I had confused Uxbridge with Richmond. After this geographical blunder had been sorted out, Didier and I arrived at the Wheatley Estate. The house was very grand, the property stretching to the edge of the Thames. The family in the story had become faded gentry, so the vast lawns and formal gardens would provide a perfect backdrop for their unreal world. We had access to enough rooms to be able to successfully portray most aspects of their lives. We reconnoitred as much as we needed on the estate, met the owners, and discussed what would happen the next day.

Stuart had gathered vintage vehicles of all kinds, bicycles and various trappings, and these arrived by degrees early on Day 1. A scene with the meet of the local hunt was scheduled for Day 3 and 4. Horses, hounds and their handlers would appear then, another element that bit substantially into the budget. With Stuart's masterful hand the chaos gradually became order until it resembled a workable set. Now we were ready to roll.

When we started shooting, Phil's camera skills were tried to the utmost. The Orangery, a superb curved building with arched windows, unfortunately gave off endless reflections. If he used polarised lenses these would give a cold haze to the film. Varying the lighting was the only answer and this took forever to achieve. The other major difficulty was depicting the distant view from the house without any vista evoking every tired cliché.

There were lighter moments to leaven the mix. Encouraged by Martin, a band of swans chased the girls along the river bank. Phil captured some hilarious footage before we were interrupted by a band of joggers on the towpath.

During Week 2 I established a routine. We would briefly rehearse then shoot, in as few takes as possible. Already, I could see that if we didn't adopt this method, panic would quickly set in. Thus, we would block with a mind to the dynamics of the scene—advance or withdrawal, threat or defence—however the rhythm of the scene demanded it. Phil worked like an automaton, one angle following another in quick succession.

Rehearsal would start with an overview of the scene. I encouraged as much improvisation as we could until we hit on what was best. Shaping the change of direction in every scene was of the greatest importance, the lines almost becoming markers in the action. If we moved from rehearsal into shooting as quickly as possible, I reasoned that the cast would forget the presence of camera and crew. When directing, I deliberately didn't say too much, simply giving praise, or asking for another take. If questions did get asked I answered them as briefly as I could. My approach to the story was to confirm every part of the action, so what was seen on screen was totally unambiguous. The extras worked well, they were focussed and almost tireless. That was good to see. Every cog in the machine was operating smoothly, or so I thought.

Quite why Phil insisted on a crane shot in the street scenes in the East End I have now forgotten. The jib arrived in the middle of the week as planned. What was not taken into account was our assistant cameraman falling from the top of the crane. Fortunately, a pile of mattresses behind a flat ready for the stuntman's scene cushioned his fall. In these enlightened days, only the camera gets hoisted in the air, operated by some very snazzy and versatile hydraulics. Not in the

Seventies—a cameraman didn't have that luxury.

The incident may have raised the emotional temperature on the set, Carrie certainly had problems with her lines afterwards. She featured in an intense exchange with Martin's character and, after the fifth take I called a break. I led Carrie to the edge of the set. We could not go far, as only half the street had been cordoned off, but it was enough.

"I can't do it the way you want it … I know it was okay in rehearsal but now … I'm so sorry."

I could see the tears.

"It's fine."

Carrie looked at me shyly.

"What d'you mean?"

"You don't have to do it that way, we'll do it differently."

"Really?"

"Just work on it together …"

Without warning Carrie threw her arms around my neck and kissed me several times.

"Oh, you're so wonderful. Thank you. Thank you."

We walked back on set holding hands. Phil looked at us in a fatherly way. After two mishaps, I was expecting a third, but the gods must have been on vacation, as it didn't happen.

By the beginning of Week 4 we were established in another of Charles' haunts—Curryfield Park in Bedfordshire. When we arrived there had been some confusion with the owners as to what parts of the property we could use, but Stuart had masterfully handled the situation. We had two weeks of intensive shooting planned and the wolves of time, if such creatures existed, were snapping at my heels. Charles and Gavin decided to visit us and stood by silently while we did a take. We then broke for lunch and I introduced Charles to Didier and Phil. They seemed a little nonplussed by him. Gavin's deference to Charles was also rather odd and he seemed more interested in what the catering truck had to offer than how his work was being interpreted on film. Charles was all smiles and encouragement.

"Everything seems to be going really well …"

"We're up against it a bit … for time I mean."

Charles looked quizzical.

"Things always take longer than you expect … stuff you just can't predict always happens."

His voice was clipped.

"But you're confident you can get it all done in time?"

"I intend to do that … on time … on budget. We just have to work a bit harder. Stuart is making miracles happen."

"Who's he? Remind me."

"Our line producer."

"Of course. Well, you seem to be in control so I'll leave you to it. I might pop in when you're getting near the end … have another chat then."

"Good idea."

Gavin reappeared at that moment, and he and Charles left together. I was surprised at how relieved I was to see them go.

* * *

Curious about Charles, I conducted a little research into his financial background, uncovering the true extent of his dealings. He had several off-shore interests and numerous companies, the bulk of which were obviously tax shelters. His network of businesses was so extensive it would have taken an army of investigators to locate them all. Whether any of his affairs were actually illegal would have been impossible to tell, but I suspected he constantly sailed close to the wind.

I didn't personally need to consult Charles about anything, as the bank updated him regularly about the outgoings of the project's funds. If I had wanted to see him in person, I was sure it would have been like seeking an audience with the Pope. It was common knowledge that Charles had an office in Pimlico where he surrounded himself with a coterie of assistants just to protect him from unwanted visitors.

We were shooting interiors in a house in Orme Square—the staircase and hall providing the setting for a grand entrance by Lord Brent, one of the main characters. Once more Charles timed his visit to coincide with lunch so we had time to chat. He had grown a beard, trimmed as to be almost invisible, and had adopted a mid-Atlantic accent.

A gofer brought our lunch out to the garden, where we were alone. I could see Charles looking around him appreciatively at the mix of technology and tradition.

"Y'know. This is something I could really have fun with …"

I was non-committal.

"I've got a great distribution deal on this movie, y'know."

I was more interested in this.

"Yeah?"

"I convinced our American friends British costume drama was going to be the next big thing on TV."

I must have looked alarmed.

"You sold it to TV?"

"To PBS over there ... that's just another outlet."

"But you're still planning to release it as a movie?"

Charles drew his chair closer.

"Oh, yes, no worries about that. In fact I've been negotiating for the best place to hold the premier."

"What did you decide?"

"It's a tossup between London, Birmingham or Edinburgh."

I wasn't convinced.

"*London* I can see ... but ..."

Charles laughed indulgently.

"Not the other two? Got to break the mould, Jack ... be innovative. That's where the movie scene is going as we come into the Eighties. I can only see the British film business taking off in a big way."

The prediction was correct; it did flourish for a time, but its swan song quickly followed.

"My business credentials give me an advantage, Jack. I look for trends and invest in them. I'm going to do more of that, and in a big way."

"I'd be very careful, if I were you. If you don't mind me saying so ..."

Charles continued to look smug.

"I don't mind you saying so ..."

"A lot of people have lost a lot of money in movies, thinking they had sure-fire winners, it turning out they didn't."

"They can't have been as clever as me then."

The conversation could go no further after a remark like that. I was also convinced Charles' next move would be to try and get me involved with other film projects. He suddenly put his hand on my arm in a way I resented.

"I've got lots more ideas for movies in mind."

I was inclined to tell him to make sure to keep them there.

"I think we ought to finish this one first don't you?"

He smiled indulgently, as if talking to a favourite nephew.

"Of course, of course ... just keep it in mind, that's all."

The wrap party was lavish enough to please even the most indulgent ligger, but I was not feeling particularly buoyant. My fee for directing was safe in the bank, but I felt like a punter who has had a lucky win. He cashes in his chips and heads out the door before the heavies start after him.

The luvvies were gathered in force around the champagne and profiteroles. Charles was nowhere to be seen. I retreated to the edge of the gathering to find Phil, looking equally out of place.

"We did pretty well on that budget y'know ... costume drama is always bloody expensive ... takes every cent."

"There's still post to do, but I'm out of that … Jeff will handle it."

Phil looked up from his plate of smoked salmon.

"It could still all get screwed up yet."

Which is exactly what happened.

You didn't get to be a millionaire several times over by being Mister Nice Guy. Charles was an investment banker, a man who did deals and I was not convinced he was ready for a significant role in the biz. Where Douglas was concerned, the pursuit of seduction was his abiding motive, but Charles appeared blind to the attractions of Venus. He was another enigma and I was more than uneasy about the fate of *Such Stuff*.

A week or two later I started hearing all was not well and, soon after that, I had sufficient reasons not to attend the premier. Pete called me, well- primed with the latest instalment in the saga.

"Problems in post I heard …"

"Enough for me to take my name off the movie."

"That bad, eh?"

"Charles … who knows absolutely fuck-all about movies *or anything else* … told Jeff he wanted *changes*."

"His company had final cut, of course …"

"*Movie Mister* certainly had that, it was in my contract. Charles didn't get what he wanted at first though. Jeff stuck to his guns, said he wasn't cutting one frame unless it was his decision to do so, and told him to piss off."

"Editors hate having a director in the cutting room. A producer? Forget it."

"He locked the doors of the editing suite and

wouldn't let Charles in."

Pete was impressed.

"Wow! Old Jeff's a hard article ..."

"In the end it didn't do him any good, of course. Charles could have got his lawyers in or whatever, and there certainly wasn't any point in me getting involved. Nothing would stop him, and in the end it got *re-edited* by some crony of his."

"Pain in the arse ..."

"The only good thing was I got paid, and so did everyone else."

"Jeff as well?"

"He always asks for his money up front these days ... exactly because of situations like that."

Pete was tooled up.

"Is he a complete nutter, this Charles bloke?"

"I think he suddenly got star struck and thought *he* was the director, or something."

I could hear Pete's long sigh.

"It happens and, with the way things are now, it'll happen even more. We are entering the era of the entrepreneur, my friend. The artist will soon be side-lined, if not made redundant. When this new government gets in, which it will I'm sure, there's going to be some big changes too. Big bucks available for bum movies."

I wasn't tuned in to the new dawn everyone was predicting.

"I wouldn't know. I just don't want my reputation, such as it is, associated with any more movies that are someone's stupid ego trip."

Whether you celebrate Christmas or not, everyone has a turkey at some time in their lives. The movie was panned so badly after the premier, the distributors took fright. American TV reneged on their agreement and *Such Stuff* sank without trace.

Later, I heard that Charles had moved out to Hollywood convinced he could take on the big boys over there. Needless to say they ate him for brunch, lunch and dinner and took *Movie Mister* for every cent it owned. LA always lives up to its reputation as being the land of dreams, nightmares as well.

Thankfully, at the beginning of the new decade things did get better. After the showing of the TV documentary on Indie Films, in which *La Mer* featured heavily, my name started being mentioned by a few people in the biz. *Kimberley Shannon*, a production company that had recently scored more than once, got in touch. When they did, playing it cool—when I wanted to jump up and down like a puppy on speed—was a distinct art.

"Are you free to come to a meeting on Thursday?"

"I think so."

"Great. Would 11 a.m. be okay for you? The production team would like to discuss the possibility of your involvement in a project we have on our books."

"I'll be there. Thanks very much."

"We look forward to meeting you, Mr. Strange."

If I had been capable of performing a somersault or two on the carpet I would have done.

The *Kimberley Shannon* offices were in Chelsea. The PA attached to Lyndon Hall, the EP, showed me into the meeting room. Introductions were quickly made—Hall, the Co-Producer Simon Chick and, to my delight, Kenny. Her star as a producer seemed to be rising. My hosts were friendly enough, although Kenny's smile was warmer. Lyndon and Simon seemed impressed that we knew each other, as if that was recommendation enough. I had the feeling they were more than relying on Kenny to ensure the production went smoothly. Simon did not cease to glance in her direction whenever he spoke. I put myself on one of the leather sofas and waited to see what might unfold.

"Okay, Jack ... the movie is a comedy adventure set in Australia ... based on a novel from over there that sold really well. It's made a good showing on the best-seller lists over here too. I think any movie of the book will go okay in the UK and in the States too."

He passed me the glossily bound screenplay. I read the title—*Beryl Billabong*. I must have looked slightly perplexed as he was quickly in there.

"You might think that's a little strange but we thought we'd go with the name of the book and use that as a working title anyway."

I nodded.

"Sounds good."

"The most important thing obviously, from your point of view, is to read the script and see if you like it. If you would consider directing the film we'd be honoured."

"Fine."

"I must say we all like your work very much, and so do a lot of other people too."

I nodded, modestly I hoped.

"We'd like a particular look to the picture, and we think you can provide that for us. I'll leave Kenny to discuss those things with you at a later date … that is if you decide to come in with us."

Kenny smiled encouragingly and Simon turned to her.

"I think we have most of the major aspects in place, don't we? Funding, locations … and today we nailed distribution I think. Is that right, Kenny?"

Kenny opened a file and studied the contents, whether just for effect I couldn't decide.

"US and UK distribution … yes. I had no problem in LA with a cast that good … they went for it straight away."

While Simon was smiling proudly, I noticed that Lyndon was looking at his watch. He rose very deliberately and looked around.

"I really do have to get that flight to New York."

The PA jumped up on cue.

"I'm sure I heard the cab guy downstairs …"

I got up too, and Lyndon shook my hand.

"Splendid to meet you, Jack. Let us know … be good to have you aboard."

"I'll be in touch as soon as I can."

"That's great. Thank you."

Lyndon and the PA left and I knew there wouldn't be much else to discuss. I glanced at the balcony that overlooked Ironsides Terrace and then at Kenny. She was definitely the best ally I could have.

Putting some time aside to study the script, I was relieved to find I liked what I read, and right from the start. By the time I had finished I wanted in. The next day I called Simon Chick and told him so. He seemed very pleased, said he had to discuss any final decision with Lyndon Hall and promised to call me. He did promptly, and a formal offer came from *Kimberley Shannon* before noon the next day. I was so elated, I forget to call Pete. He would find out sooner or later, I knew that. He would tease me about it, and quite right too.

I thought about Kenny and knew she would probably be ready with a sly dig as well. That was why I was glad to have her and Pete about the place; they kept my feet firmly on the ground. I had always liked the way Kenny didn't waste any time discovering what anyone had to offer and if she wanted to work with them. She did call later, to offer her congratulations.

"I did put in a good word for you, but basically they liked you from the off."

"Thanks, anyway."

"What did you think of the script … *honestly*."

"It's okay … *really*. Simple story … ugly duckling who blooms into a star."

"You think that's all there is to it?"

"Whoever wrote it was fascinated by the supposed glamour of showbiz … it's the Australian equivalent of Las Vegas I guess."

"I can't believe how cynical you are, Jack! Such a poignant tale … one full of deep meaning."

"So is sex … or can be."

"That's true."

I decided to be serious.

"Kenny, I wouldn't have agreed to direct unless I thought we could do something with it. We've got a great cast, the locations look fine …"

"I know what you mean. It has enough subtlety … slightly subversive … in the end reassuringly mainstream for the market. That's how they got the backing, it must have been."

There was one of those pauses that I soon began to associate with Kenny—loaded.

"Can I be utterly honest about you as director?"

"Sure, go ahead."

"You've got to have a top-notch AD with you."

"I know, I thought that too … for something this big."

Kenny was quick to be reassuring, without losing any ground.

"It's not that I doubt your talents in any way, I wouldn't have suggested you to them if I thought that. It's just there's mega-money riding on this. If we screw up for any reason, or get behind schedule there's going to be big trouble for me. So, by having a good AD around you, that's much less likely."

"Who have we got for that…?"

Kenny reading from a list.

"The AD I want is Adrian Janes. We've got camera Toby Mills, sound Tony Camely …"

"Don't tell me any more names, I'll only forget them straightaway."

"Silly boy! Do you want to know about locations, or are you going to forget where those are as soon as I tell you?"

"I promise to listen closely to those, they'll be easy to remember."

"The sets are being built in a huge hangar, duplicating for Oz, so we don't have any location stuff at all!"

"Tease!"

"I know. Their idea is to whack every bit of the budget into the dancing extravaganzas."

"There's a country house bit though isn't there? Funny, because not that long ago we shot at a couple of those."

"Obviously you're the man for the job then. You're right, it's only three days ... at Lilley Park near Farnham."

Kenny picked up on my thoughts.

"What's on your mind?"

"There is quite a surreal episode isn't there?"

"The beach at night with the lights and everything? They were going to do that with animation."

I sighed.

"Yeah, I suppose all that stuff is a lot *less* tacky now, but I reckon we could try something else."

"Like what?"

"Ever been to Brighton?"

"Once or twice."

"The beach has a strange look at night with all the lights along the front shining on the water. I don't know whether we could catch that. There's also the Pavilion ... could be worth looking into."

"Okay, let's check it out sometime. Anything else?"

"Not that I can think of. I reckon it'll work, I really do ..."

"Yeah, I have a good feeling about it too."

* * *

Having an AD that produced a shot list at the beginning of each day was a great luxury. Add a storyboard artist and I was in heaven. Such tight organisation was essential as the action was mainly the dance numbers. Romantic involvement and show-biz politics provided some respite from the frantic choreography. Light and shade had to be in there somewhere with a few scenes being deliberately slow-paced.

At first, I missed having Phil around but I soon realised Toby's straight-forward style suited the movie. When filming any interaction between the actors, he favoured over the shoulder shots combined with them moving forward to their marks. With such a professional cast, this kind of sequence worked easily. I was sure tight framing was important too, giving enough visual variation in the dialogue. I didn't want an audience getting restless during those parts of the film, merely waiting for the next dance sequence to begin. Before digital arrived, when a monitor now enables a director to check the image before shooting, every shot was framed within the camera. In retrospect, I am certain this factor strengthened the bond between director and cameraman.

Toby was adept at varying his choice of lenses and we agreed that deep focus shots were essential in some of the dance sequences, so as to give drama before the movement began. This put the production designer on his mettle as every detail of the set had to be in place; there could be no skimping. I was certain we needed to be that meticulous too; *Kimberley Shannon* would be looking for the money shots before anything else.

Although I had done all my homework and prepared the first day's shooting as much as I could, there were still moments on set when I was at a loss. Convinced that if the crew smelt fear I would be easy prey, I was perhaps more abrupt than I should have been. Adrian took me aside when we were having a break in the morning.

"Can I just say something?"

"I wish you would."

He smiled in friendly fashion.

"*Relax*, that's all. Nobody's going to bite you, even if you do goof up. Everyone might think you more human if you did that anyway."

"Yeah, you're right. Thanks, I needed to hear that."

I very quickly learned how to make an easy request, and when to insist on something without sounding dictatorial. Luckily, I rarely needed to exert any authority as I had such a willing and understanding crew. Having a plan did not mean it was set in stone, and they appreciated I was always prepared to listen to a different approach.

As always, time was tight—six weeks, which amounted to thirty shooting days. I had anticipated we would need three days for the exterior shoot in Farnham and I was allowing two days for my night experiments in Brighton. The rest of the time we were confined to the aircraft hangar.

It was a revelation to discover that filming with forty background actors was not that much different from dealing with three or four. As long as the AD made sure everyone was focused and listening to instructions, it all went smoothly. For the action pieces I put in two extra cameras. I knew this would mean additional lighting, but I was convinced we needed every bit of footage we could get. When I told Kenny about my intentions, she protested at first, but eventually agreed and the rushes vindicated my decision.

I also wanted to use a steadi-cam operator. This technology was so new it wasn't easy to find. More importantly, someone competent to operate it was just as hard to track down. Kenny persisted and eventually we got who we needed. The shots were almost revolutionary, putting the movie way ahead of its contemporaries. Smooth footage of the crowd antics during the set pieces, shot almost from floor level, was a real visual bonus when it came to editing.

After we had finished filming the dance finale that came at the end of the movie, I was far more at ease. Up until then, worrying about the next day's arrangements had given me sleepless nights. Kenny had also lost the tense expression she wore in the first few weeks of shooting. We even agreed to have a drink together one Friday evening.

The King and Prince was the nearest pub to the location and also in the direction we would both take back to London. Kenny flopped down at a table while I went to the bar and returned with our drinks.

"Cheers."

"Yes, Cheers! Here's to great success, which I'm sure it will be."

"I certainly hope so, Kenny, and I'm very grateful to have such a veteran at my side."

"God, you make me sound so ancient."

"No, just experienced."

Kenny laughed.

"Now I'm some raddled old tart!"

"Sorry, I'm obviously getting all my words wrong tonight."

She squeezed my hand reassuringly.

"You're doing fine."

We sipped in silence for a moment.

"*Kimberley Shannon* gave me a brief on you, but it didn't tell me anything much I didn't know already. Since I last saw you … what have you done? *Such Stuff* … was that it?"

"Best forgotten, that one."

Kenny shrugged.

"Never mind, you made it onto this one."

"I think I only got this because of *La Mer* … I was some kind of hip, director who had once won at Cannes and might add kudos to the whole business."

Kenny looked moderately stern.

"Don't knock it. *La Mer* was thought of very highly. I was the one who the *Palme D'or* actually got handed to, remember. People were talking about that movie for ages."

"Yeah, I was flavour of the month for a bit, although it's taken nearly ten years to get my first real feature."

"It just took time …"

I mused briefly.

"That would never have happened at all if Douglas hadn't found the money for *La Mer*, you know."

"He must have thought you were okay about him

152

… after he fell out with everyone else."

"I quite liked him."

I could see Kenny studying me.

"You know I had an affair with Douglas a few years ago … around the time we did *La Mer*."

"Wasn't there somebody else …"

I wished I hadn't said it, particularly when Kenny came back at me.

"*There were lots of somebody elses!* He might as well have given us all numbers! I think he even made a play for your French piece …"

"Martine. Yes, he did … she told me."

I braced myself for a full-scale assault on the male sex, with me being the nearest representative.

"He dumped me for that Lady Claverham-Whatsit. I think he's going to marry her now. Good luck to the woman, she'll bloody need it coping with a cock-artist like that."

Her bitterness was like a rising tide.

"What's he doing now?"

"Actually, Douglas is doing pretty well in TV. I think they wanted him as a figurehead, really, respectability … that sort of thing."

"On what?"

"He's producing *Sam Edison* … the detective series. Set in Cambridge … Bill Frost is the star."

I shook my head

"I haven't seen it … don't seem to watch much telly these days."

"You will do. You'll end up *working* in television. We all have to at some time or another."

I said nothing, but it didn't seem to matter.

Being in Kenny's company was pleasant enough, and I looked at her once or twice in an appraising way. Women always know when this is happening. Men, mostly being dull, don't think they do.

"I always said I'd never have a relationship with someone in the biz …"

Was this a double-bluff?

"No, probably wise."

Kenny toyed with the glass in front of her.

"The trouble is we fall in love, don't we? Or we think we do. I would have done anything for Douglas."

She looked away, as if some memory was too much for her to recall.

"God, he was incredible in bed."

I was never quite sure what that meant. The first time a friend of mine talked about his girlfriend being 'great in bed' I burst out laughing. I wondered what accomplishments she had under the covers. Making tea, or solving a crossword puzzle?

Life is constant change; we make decisions and respond to situations. Acting attempts to mimic how life really is. Cathy, who played Beryl's best friend Noelene in the movie, struggled with what was not an easy part. Noelene is also the ex-girlfriend of Bruce, the guy who is Beryl's true love. Beryl, however, is convinced that she is not attractive enough to catch Bruce's eye. Noelene must be seen to take on enough angst for both of them. Because of her own wacky nature the turmoil wavers constantly between tragedy and comedy.

Gemma, who played Beryl, showed only the most

minimal of inflections. To make it all work, Cathy had to do something different. In the scene we were about to shoot, Noelene has to show that her emotions are changing so rapidly that from shot to shot she has to be different every time. Even a very seasoned actor would have had to draw on all their skills. I detected that a little private tuition was required.

"Look, I know what they teach you in drama school ... to bring out the emotion from inside and all that, but I'm not sure that's going to work here."

Cathy shook her hair about.

"Yeah, like you can see the joins ... I know what you mean."

"It's best if you focus on some word, keeping that in your head. That way you make the whole thing constant, or else it's going to look too bitty. Go through the whole scene giving *clues* all the time as to what *you're* feeling. Let Beryl do her own stuff. Don't react, almost as if you're not listening to what she's saying."

"I think I know what you mean. So when you see her, you realise that Noelene's problems are just as important as Beryl's."

I nodded briefly.

"Exactly. The attention is bound to be on Beryl because she's the main character so we've got to find a way to *bring you up* at certain points. I can do that in camera, or with both your moves, but I don't want to make it too obvious. I'd rather what happens between you two actually tells the story."

Cathy looked better about it all.

"Okay, I see."

"We can always try different things. I'll just say 'that's crap' when it doesn't work."

Cathy gave me a mean look.

"You do that and I'll slap you round the chops."

We both started laughing and falling about, holding onto each other. The AD appeared right at that moment.

"We're ready to go."

Cathy smoothed down her hair.

"Yeah, I got the first word in my head too."

"Good."

"It's 'crap.'"

I winked at her.

"I can tell it'll be fine."

And it was.

When Kenny called on the weekend I knew there was something wrong. This was before she even started to speak.

"They're insisting we *do* go to Australia now!"

"Oh, no! Who had that stupid idea?"

"I think it has to be the studio."

I tried to calm her.

"They'll forget it about it, believe me."

"Will they?"

"Someone along the line will remind them of the simple fact that if they film in Australia they lose all the tax concessions they're getting here. My mate Pete happened to be telling me all about these things only the other day."

"I can't understand why they even considered it."

"Somebody piped up at one of those *studio*

conferences, and they thought it was great idea."

Kenny was still a touch doomy.

"I wonder if Simon has that much actual say in what goes on. There's so much studio money tied up, *and* TV money from their subsidiaries in America."

"Right, but they went to Kimberley … here in the UK … because of all these tax-deferred advantages. That must mean something."

Kenny appeared to agree.

"True, and I'll tell you something else too … the studio have decided they want to do a whole bunch of productions here. Now they've got you, they think that's dead handy."

"And all the time there's me thinking it was because I'm such a great director …"

"Well, you're not bad …"

"So generous and encouraging …"

"Idiot! I do know, as well, the distribution in Oz was sewn up before the script was even finished. They wanted to cash in on the book being so popular. Getting investment in America was a piece of cake too, I knew that when I went to LA. It's in profit already."

"What about Lyndon, our jet-setting EP? How does he figure in all this?"

"You saw him, Jack, Mr. Faceless in the VIP lounge with his executive briefcase … having free drinks in business class."

I was now resolved.

"Okay, here's what we do. We just say we don't think it's a good idea. They won't fire us, it's too far down the road. I bet they'll think of something else later on even sillier."

They did try it on again too, but thankfully not until we'd finished shooting.

Lilley Park felt as if it was a long way from any suburban sprawl. We were there to shoot a few scenes with Beryl among the nobs, her supposedly charming gaucherie in their company. All was going well until the sound man started kicking up. Apparently no one had noticed the dual carriageway, concealed from the front of the house but quite visible—and audible— from the other side. How the location manager had overlooked this nightmare was slightly baffling. It meant setting the scene some way from the house. As a feature in the background it looked okay on camera, but seemed less than the best use of a no doubt pricy location.

My experiment on the shore in Brighton tried Toby's power of invention, but he went along with it. By using an 85mm lens he captured the alien quality I wanted. The 35mm took in the close ups of flashing ripples on the sea. With double exposure we combined the two sets of lights and create a kaleidoscope of colour, one edged with silver. It worked.

The camaraderie that accompanies a successful production turns into melancholy at the wrap party. Like a holiday romance, it's all over—none of us may ever meet again. Our own personal triumph has become yet another illusion, accolades bestowed by a fickle god.

I was jocular enough with everyone, genuinely pleased with all that had been achieved, though with the apprehension that post had yet to get underway. Kenny and I exchanged smiles and hugs, but my real glances were reserved for someone else. Barbara had appeared from nowhere at the party, apparently unaccompanied. I honed in on her straight away and from the start she welcomed my attentions. As soon as I was able, I captured her and we sped off to Fulham. As soon as we got into the flat she shed her fur wrap and put her arms around me.

"I'm being a good girl and keeping my promise aren't I? Now we can try the bed."

Barbara undressed speedily, and lay there watching me, her eyes sparkling.

"C'mon, darling, I'm all ready and waiting for you …"

I was hard and excited, I had been wanting her for so long. The way she parted her legs as wide as she did, I had no option but to climb aboard. If being inside Barbara was not paradise, then I would be quite content with whatever was happening right then. She encouraged me to try every which way of taking her, and I did so. Pumping her hard, then slowly grinding, and from every angle I could think of. I was making up for lost time, and when we eventually slid between the sheets we would not let each other rest. All through the night we loved each other until we eventually fell asleep. At dawn I was woken by a whisper.

"Who's a little raver then?"

I didn't say anything, just put her underneath me and started again. Barbara locked her legs round my neck and I plunged deeper and deeper into her once more.

11

My sex-life might have reached a super high, but there was little to celebrate elsewhere. The rough cut for *Billabong* was rough alright—like a dog's nuts. I couldn't understand why this had happened as we had more than enough excellent footage. What the editor had offered us was just a disjointed series of scenes that had as much resemblance to a movie as a flick-book. Doubt crept in and quickly became a toxic flood. Why did it look such a mess? Kenny was also totally at a loss when she called.

"This guy is top of the range that's why I hired him in the first place, but he just isn't getting it."

Problems with editors seemed to be the bane of my movie career.

"What I've seen so far is just depressing … there's no life … thread … nothing."

Kenny was almost wailing.

"So what are we going to do?"

"One word …"

"What's that?"

"*Who's that* … Jeff."

"The guy who did *La Mer*?"

"Right, the one I owe my career to, really."

"I thought you said that was Douglas …"

160

"Glad the humour banks are still charged up, sweetie."

Kenny breathed, hard.

"Only just, this is serious."

"Will the budget handle us getting Jeff in?"

"Depends for how long. The studio *ought* to play ball, we did come in way under budget …"

"And on time. That still ought to count for something."

Kenny deliberated, but not for long.

"Just do it … go for it. I'll sweet talk Simon and Lyndon. I'll have to be pretty subtle, I don't them thinking it's a disaster or they'll panic."

"I'm sure you'll succeed. Remember, desperate times need desperate measures…."

"Really. I can handle *Kimberley Shannon* … at least … their London Office … I don't know about LA."

"Okay, I'll get Jeff onto to it … if I can."

By yet another miracle I did get hold of Jeff. He was rapidly assuming the role of trouble-shooter in my own film world. Having got over this, Kenny and I were less than joyous to be summoned to a meeting at Ironside Terrace. When I was informed this was a 'strategy conference' I enquired bluntly as to what that was, but the Lyndon's PA was deliberately vague. Kenny and I exchanged a brief word in the morning, but were both in the dark as to what was likely to happen.

We arrived in Chelsea to find Simon and Lyndon with a duo of dudes who were totally unfamiliar. They looked as if they were studio reps, one having a strong New York accent and a too-firm handshake, the other weasely and annoying. Simon was at his most diplomatic.

"There have been a few suggestions made about changes in the project ..."

A studio issuing directives during production can be challenged. In post production it usually spells disaster—advice being offered by those who know less than zero, and decisions being made that should never even have been suggested. My heart sank to somewhere lower than my socks. The first item on the agenda was the title of the movie. I waited as a sheet was handed to Simon; he read this out almost in sepulchral tones.

"*Super Sheila* ... *Spunky Sheila* ... *Saucy Sheila*."

Both Kenny and I sat unmoved, Simon looking more and more embarrassed. I stepped in.

"*Billabong* is the title of the book, so everyone knows that already. If Australia is going to be our main market then, surely, messing with it can't be a good plan. Frankly, those ideas we've heard will be seen as patronising to an Oz audience. *Beryl Billabong* is a good title, it suits the character, it's very Australian ... suits the ambiance. I think we've even got an original genre."

Mr. New York made some point about the movie's transatlantic appeal. Simon looked over at Kenny; I quickly realised she wasn't nearly as confident when dealing with these kind of suits, but she still said her piece.

"I spent a lot of time in LA sounding out people's

opinions, and not just any old studio-exec either. All the responses I got to the project pre-production were positive, so much so that we wanted to get into shooting before someone ripped off the idea."

The Weasel made a few noises at this point, questioning this assessment. I was gratified to see that Lyndon supported Kenny.

"Kenny is absolutely right. I did my own fact-finding exercise in and around the studios over there, and the money men … that's where you always find the shrewdest take on the upcoming trends … tell me that Kenny has definitely got it right."

Mr. New York made a remark which implied that, despite all this, he and Weasel just had to know best. Based on what evidence was not made clear. Kenny became flustered and I could see she was very tired. I defended her views once more and, to their credit, Kenny and Lyndon upped the ante and said they were right behind me. The trump card was that a hastily-arranged screening of *La Mer* had been warmly received when it was shown to a select group of the studio hierarchy the previous evening. Someone was a big fan of the movie on the West Coast; maybe the San Francisco guy was still rooting for me after all this time! The upshot of this was that the studio had 100% confidence in me as a director and Kenny as producer. We were a winning team—as far as they were concerned that was all they needed to know.

The execs looked much put out, as if they had been let down by the home team. Obviously California had not briefed them on this development. The eight hour time difference might have worked in our favour in a strange way. Weasel admitted defeat and they both peremptorily got up to leave. Simon was looking concernedly at Kenny. He suggested she go and lie down in the ante room next door. She agreed and I indicated I would go with her.

The room was sparsely furnished, the main item being a wide sofa, what, in the bad old days, would have been regarded as a 'casting couch'. Kenny and I sat together on this, and as soon as the door was closed she sobbed uncontrollably in my arms. I held her until she informed me she felt just about human again. She stood up and straightened her outfit.

"Come on, we don't want them to think we've been bonking in here."

Women have such a professional approach to everything.

Having fought off the studio successfully, we awaited the outcome of Jeff's hand-to-hand combat with the movie footage. Two weeks later he announced that we had a cut that was acceptable, and after another week's work there was a version that was worthy to be shown to the studio. As soon as we saw this we knew we had our movie. Kenny and I were convinced it worked. *Billabong* happened because Jeff's editing was snappy and convincing, I had coaxed some great performances out of the actors, and everything was right there on the screen, where it counts.

Inevitably, Simon had to cope with yet more carping from the cooks stirring the broth at the Studio. Mr. X would bluster and Mr. Y was shown to be talking out of his backside—the usual stuff. Kenny and I stood firm and resolutely refused to even consider any more changes. We were proved right when the movie was released. *Billabong* was the biggest success of the mid-eighties. It made the studio a better return than they could have ever anticipated, and the movie was hailed as a stylish piece of entertainment, earning a lot of critical acclaim. We were nominated for the BAFTA awards and, although we lost out to some worthless Hollywood confection, that gave our movie even more kudos.

The figures said it all. For a budget of ten million we grossed eight times that amount. The studio hadn't predicted such a profit and neither had the movie pundits. I recalled William Goldman's words written in that same year. He said, referring to the biz, 'Nobody knows anything'. You got it, Bill. They don't know Sweet FA, any of 'em.

My director's fee, and a wisely negotiated gross point of half a percent, earned me more money than I had ever known. After some deliberation, I decided to move out of London and back to Barstowe. I found a fine Georgian house at No. 37 Richardson Gardens in Clinton, one which would be my home for the next thirty years. I would only ever travel to London when work forced me to. When I called Pete he was his usual sardonic self.

"Who's got a big man now then, eh? Hollywood next?"

"Not yet …"

"If you do get out there, don't go the way of your little mate Charlie …"

"Charles Fry?"

"One and the same. He got involved with some bigger sharks than himself and they picked him clean."

"I heard. So what else is new?"

"I'll tell you. Home video. That is going to be huge."

"Makes sense. Why pay to go to the cinema if you can stay home and watch a movie?"

"Exactly, and once you've got the video *recorder*, you can tape anything you want off the TV Watch this space, matey … I'm telling you …"

I was looking at the world around me too, wondering what would manifest next for me.

For my parents to share in any fame I enjoyed was something I had always wanted. I arranged to meet them for lunch in the village pub to celebrate the success of the movie, but from the off I knew things were not right. My father did not look well, and was obviously not at ease in the surroundings. I strongly suspected he did not move very far from his armchair at home. My mother had visibly diminished in stature, and her lined features indicated she spent most of her time ministering to him.

Conversation, such as it was, neither sparkled nor cheered. My triumphs had come too late for them to participate in, or even understand. Slowly, the occasion meandered to its conclusion. Wishing them well, I departed for Barstowe, somewhat troubled at heart.

* * *

Leaving London meant I saw less and less of Barbara and she eventually disappeared from my life. At the premier of *Billabong* when she was on my arm, we had definitely been an item. Barbara loved glamour and success as much as she did sex, and in pursuit of both she took up with a new beau in California. I resigned myself to sleeping solo for the immediate future. It did not take long, however, before I was involved with someone new.

Of all my relationships, hooking up with Jane was possibly the most inexplicable. She was eminently conservative, perhaps reflecting my becoming a man of property and, at the same time, celebrating my fortieth birthday. Did I want to put down roots? At first, I liked to walk around the new house and buy a bit of furniture here and there, but the novelty soon wore off. Whatever prompted this sea change, after less than a year of knowing each other, Jane and I were engaged. If that sounds as if I was not the one who suggested the union, you might well be right.

With this new arrangement came a social life entirely monopolised by Jane's friends. My own small circle had been determined by the biz, formal get-togethers weren't part of the erratic routine of any of us. This new arrangement was all very different, almost alien. Lunch in a country pub every weekend, theatres and concert going, and an endless round of dinner parties. These last get-togethers should definitely have sounded a warning. I soon discovered Jane was prone to mingling with figures from the past I had cheerfully forgotten. So I was reunited with Bonzo Hinton and his chums—endless evenings that always culminated in an awful silence around the dinner table. The moment arrives when everyone realises just how much wine they have drunk, and the more sensible review their approach to the rest of the evening, while the incorrigible start anew.

Convinced that the success of Billabong meant I could sit back and let the offers roll in I relaxed—too much. With Mrs. Thatcher at the helm, the Eighties in England were a time when every day was a feast. Not many slices of pie came my way and, before I knew it, the decade was over. All that came out of it for me was a prompting to write a novel. It being my first venture into the literary life, I made every possible mistake the first-time author makes. After hurling my initial attempt into the bin where it belonged, I embarked upon a second version. Its successor was some improvement but still needed ruthless editing. After rewriting more than two thirds of the manuscript I produced *Paper Sun*—a work I was not ashamed to submit to a publisher.

The theme was the timeless quest—the notion that the Grail when eventually discovered was almost worthless, the journey being all. The theme had been dramatised before, and many times, but the irony in my story had its essence in the Holy Vessel being symbolised by the filmic masterpiece that I wanted to create. I alluded to this by contrasting the modern and the Medieval world as much as my writing skills would allow.

The first publisher I approached—Hooper-Swan— did not reply, so I tried Dormer Press. This time I included a fulsome CV, a move which turned out to be somewhat fortuitous. The novel was initially rejected as being 'not literary enough' by the editor Leon Gatwick. I shrugged this off, wondering if authorship was not a vocation I should contemplate. Thus, I was surprised to be contacted a week later by the owner of the Press.

Owen Day was a celebrated author himself, upon esoteric subjects. He had noted my credentials in the biz and wrote me a fulsome letter detailing his ideas for filming a series of occult yarns. A copy of his most recent work arrived in the next day's post. It was very apparent Day desired to see his work on the small screen, or any screen. Offering a transparent bribe—he would publish my novel if I could bring this about—I spent some time contemplating the matter.

I knew very little about the occult; my only consideration was whether the material possessed any commercial appeal. When I examined *Pagan Piper*, as the collection was titled, I could see, however, that all the necessary aspects for a drama were in place. I responded positively to Day's communication, promising to set wheels in motion for production in the New Year. Within two days a contract arrived for *Paper Sun*.

On the first day of January my father died. A man who could not accept change in the world, for him it was always 1936. He was probably among those who railed at Mrs. Simpson that year. After the war he went from military service to the civil equivalent and stayed there until he retired. I remember, as a child, he built an enormous model railway layout in the stables that were part of my grandfather's property. It was quite obvious my father preferred that I didn't touching the engines, the coaches or any of the rolling stock. Accepting this decision with some rancour, I never really forgave him. His attitude caused a deep rift between us, one that was never healed. I was aloof with him from that moment on. Sometimes I wondered if he ever knew the reason.

The funeral was a grim affair, a grey, storm-filled day ensuring that an irrevocable gloom pervaded the interior of the church. Having attended a few funerals in my life, I have never quite seen the purpose of displaying the coffin so prominently in the nave. What possible significance can a corpse have? Whether it is ripped and twisted on the battlefield, or lying in state for the populace to file reverently past, it is an empty husk. The life within has passed to another place, the details of which are a matter for theologians to squabble over. The spirit, the eternal fire of creation, remains eternal, totally indifferent to the material world.

During the brief service I reflected on whether one generation unfailingly scars the one that follows. The greatest crime they perpetrate is the lies our parents tell us concerning the nature of existence. They may have no malicious intent, but it might have been easier if they left us to make up our own minds. With the dawn of intelligence, I realised that my father and mother entertained a misguided view of the world. For this they could not be wholly condemned, it was merely the sum of their own perceptions. They were no more misguided than the teachers or other authority figures I encountered in my childhood. My parents had given me the gift of life, for that I was grateful. Being obliged to learn the ways of the universe on my own gave me no regrets.

My mother never fully recovered from the blow of my father's death and rapidly deteriorated. I soon had the thankless task of selling the family home and installing her in a nursing home. A few months later she joined my father, which was probably her dearest wish from the moment she lost him.

12

After being involved with the weedy medieval epic in the early Seventies, I had vowed never to work again in television. The recession hitting hard twenty years later changed my mind about all that. My capital began to dwindle alarmingly and there was nothing for it but to offer my services to the goggle box. Ultimately, Kenny had been right.

The wave of 'alternative' comedy that had begun at the end of the Eighties was now approaching its peak. One of the TV channels was more alert to the trend than its rivals. The programme planners had commissioned a pilot show featuring performances by the emerging stars of 'stand-up'. When it was completed, no one quite knew what to do with it.

In the years that had elapsed since its release, *Billabong* had gained a reputation as a classic comedy. Thus, my name was suggested as a possible director for the show. When a definite offer was made, I immediately accepted. The programme was being made in the same Barstowe studios I had known decades before.

Along with the producer Percy Allerton and the programme planner, I watched the pilot in the comfort of the viewing suite. Someone, with stunning originality, had named it *Helluva Laugh*. It certainly didn't live up to the title. As the end credits rolled I turned to my newly-found colleagues to gauge their reactions. The expression on their features told me all I wanted to know.

"I think we can do better than that."

"I should jolly well hope so too."

The programme-planner stared at me over the top of his glasses.

"Yes … it did rather give the impression they didn't know much about what they were filming."

He and his colleague looked at me enquiringly.

"So what do you suggest?"

"A bit of research first. Get to the places where this is really happening. London obviously, and I would guess Manchester, same as where the new music is coming from right now."

"Okay, let's see if we can get finance for a fact-finding trip …"

I smiled secretly—the usual sub-committee jargon.

"I think we should take a crew at the same time …"

Mr. Glasses noted this.

"Could do. I'll propose that at the meeting as well."

I turned to Allerton.

"There were two of those comics who looked the most interesting I thought …"

"Which ones?"

"Lord Biro and Wye Bredon."

"Where are they based?"

"One's in Wales, I think they said, the other might

even be here in Barstowe."

The programme planner started to look anxiously in my direction.

"If I can get the go-ahead, can you start straightaway? I know the high-ups are champing at the bit. Anxious not to get pipped at the post by anyone else …"

"Sure, anytime you want."

At the beginning of the next week we were en route to Manchester. Driving up the M6 in a small convoy of TV company vehicles, stuffed with crew and gear we went. This was the pioneering spirit, one I applauded. The only brief I had been given was to film as many members of an audience in the throes of hysterical laughter as I could find. The talent of the actual comics appeared to be a secondary consideration.

By ensuring that the standard of performance was as high as we could get, we made *Helluva Laugh* a success. High viewing figures were achieved, which always pleases the hierarchy. Allerton and I made a good team, and we quickly became the golden boys of that year. That acclaim, however, took its toll on me in other ways.

Within six months, the combined effects of a too comfortable relationship and working for an institution with a subsidised bar, meant that I had gained more weight than was good for me. Having a hefty lunch and two or three pints was a habit not easy to break. I was certain that the atmosphere in the TV studios prompted me to take refuge in alcohol and mindless scoffing. There was no edge or urgency in any part of the production process, and the presence of so many timeservers and jobsworths ultimately numbed the brain.

If my daytime activities were in a state of somnolence, the rest of my life was even more so. Jane worked on making the social round never ending with the result that I ended up drinking even more. She had a high-powered job in marketing which took her to Europe—Brussels mostly—during the week. I tried to stay sober while she was away, but this was a losing battle. Jane flew into the airport late on Friday night, we had dinner and drunken sex, then the usual Saturday night engagement, followed by a pub lunch on Sunday. I could not help but notice that we now almost exclusively hob-nobbed with Bonzo Hinton and various other five-star bores.

My contract as director of *Helluva Laugh* was not to be renewed, the high-ups deciding that the programme should be quietly laid to rest. If I was going to stick around in broadcast television, I had to move quickly. When I was initially signed up by the TV Company I had felt honour bound to inform Owen Day that plans for *Pagan Piper* would have to be put on hold. Now I was free to begin negotiations on his behalf. To this end, I contacted Pete to discover if he knew somebody who knew somebody else, as is the way of things in such an organisation. The TV Company was so compartmentalised that even those working in the office next to mine were unknown to me. Pete was, as always, succinct.

"The first thing you've got to do is set up your own production company. That's what they want these days. There's hardly any company produced programmes, that's so they can blame you if anything goes wrong."

"Okay, so I work independently, but still get funded by the company."

"Right. Put up a project for consideration … cost it … make sure you charge 'em for everything, including the tea bags. The bigger the budget the more they'll be impressed. They'll think they're on to a classy show then."

I noted all this carefully.

"When you get going, you have to know which internal memos to ignore and which to pay attention to, that's very important."

"How d'you tell the difference?"

"Anything that's trivial, make a big deal about answering it …"

I was blank.

"Why's that?"

"Because it's come from the head of some committee that doesn't have anything better to do except nit-pick … and they're always the ones with the say so."

Pete was right. The real power in the TV Company lay with a sorry lot of suits. Their greatest zeal was shown in assigning new working parties to sub-committees during meetings.

"They left us alone most of the time with *Helluva Laugh*. Still had to do a bit of ducking and diving to get round all those the rules and regulations … that took us more time than planning the actual programmes."

"What is it you want to get going, anyway?"

"*Pagan Piper.*"

"Is that the mystical stuff you were telling me about? For God's sake get some tits and arse in there … witches in scanty robes that sort of thing."

"I'll bear it in mind …"

"Best of luck … and stick with that producer bloke you had last time too … the one on *Helluva Laugh* … Percy Allerton. That bloke's got his feet under the table over there definitely."

By doing everything Pete suggested and with a lot of luck, someone decided *Pagan Piper* was a commercial product. I negotiated a contract which was as generous as I could expect. At the beginning of 1999 I was commissioned to direct three series of '*Pagan Piper*'—one per year. I was feeling financially secure for the first time since the Eighties.

A week later, an unexpected call from Allerton nearly threw me. Apparently, someone in charge was not convinced that '*Pagan Piper*' would attract a large enough viewing audience. I panicked.

"What about the contract?"

"Don't worry about that."

"*Say that again …*"

"It won't be affected at all, Jack. The plan is they'll still make each of the series for the three years … same shooting schedule but not give them any air time."

"How does that work?"

"They'll put them straight onto this new commercial format they've got now. They've already set up a division in the company for marketing it."

"DVD ... the thing replacing video ... or so they hope."

"I'm impressed. You're obviously no technophobe."

"Don't be cheeky ..."

Allerton laughed.

"Believe me, plenty of people who work in TV wouldn't know a format from a fruitcake."

I reflected briefly.

"It doesn't really make any difference whether it's shown on telly or not. Apart from the write-ups I suppose."

"Probably a blessing in disguise for you, I'm assuming you don't want to be associated with TV forever ... at this stage in your career."

"What career? I thought I had one once, I'm not so sure now."

"You're talking like you're middle-aged."

"I feel like it sometimes these days."

I was very definitely the wrong side of fifty, and staring at the onset of impending maturity with a resentful eye.

"We're going to use *film* by the way ... 35mm."

Now that was good news. I had dreaded the idea of using video. At this stage of the game a video image was only good enough for football matches and weddings. I later found out the DOP was an *Avengers* fan and he knew that all the best episodes—the ones with Diana Rigg—were shot on film. Hearing this, I suggested we renamed the series 'Mrs. Peel's Pagan Piper'. Not wanting the quip to get back to Owen Day, I made sure it went no further.

* * *

Anyone who wishes to chart the rise and fall of *Pagan Piper* would be best served by examining the memos received during the series. Pete had been quite right in assessing inter-departmental communications. At first they could be safely parried, because they had no relevance or bite. By the time we got to the third series I would have had to agree with most of the critical comments.

At first the scripts had been written solely by Day. In the second series a collaborator had been brought in and, towards the end, they were put together by a team. These last efforts were uniformly predictable, repeating the metaphysical themes Day had written in the first series. The plots were very thin and, worst of all, lacked any imagination. Getting in fresh writers might have stopped the rot, but it was too late. I simply gritted my teeth and counted the days till the end. My enthusiasm for shooting in graveyards at dawn, and in crypts at night had definitely waned. There had also been too much 'standing around by standing stones', as the AD so wittily put it.

In retrospect I was amazed *Pagan Piper* had garnered the DVD sales that it did. The New Age was dawning, and an obsession with all things mystical and metaphysical had brought new punters at a moment when interest might well have flagged.

At the end of 2003 I parted company with the television company for good.

I had seen for myself the insidious effect TV had on enthusiasm, talent and my waistline. The dreariness of the canteen and the overheated social club produced a race of studio-bound zombies.

Quite where my life in movies would lead next I could not anticipate. I figured I was capable of working in the biz for the next ten years, and I was determined to make that count. What had happened to the ambition that had driven me to make *La Mer*? That all seemed an age or more away. I had grown flabby, and my attitude to life was stale. Finally rebelling against the shackles of society, I patently refused to attend any more of the social events Jane organised. Naturally this caused domestic friction, but she responded by attending these events alone. I was relieved to stay at home and, by consummate will-power, I stayed sober as well. Occasionally though, I did venture out.

I accepted an invitation to attend the premiere of *Journey in a Shallow Place* at the Dobson Arts Centre and duly turned up before the show. The director—Conway Gibson—looked permanently glum, only altering his expression when he was talking airily about his 'many projects in development'. Such a term was universally regarded in the biz as an indication of failure. Either you were working or you weren't. Suggesting that you might be didn't mean diddly-squat.

Rumour had it that Gibson could not find a distributor and had hired the venue himself to show his movie. The usual crowd of freeloaders and wannabes that such events attract were in attendance. I wandered into the bar and stood around looking for anyone I knew. This was not the usual movie crowd, just a random selection of Saturday night revellers. That alone spoke volumes about the movie. While ordering a bottle of over-priced lager I was aware of someone beside me.

"Hi. Are you Jack Strange, by any chance?"

Being recognised has the effect of flattering anyone, unless you're so famous you try to avoid it. I hadn't qualified for the permanent Raybans league quite yet.

"That's right. How's it going?"

"Great, really great. Ed Levi. Good to meetcha."

I took the hand speedily extended in my direction, and noted the West Coast twang.

"Loved yer movie *Billabong*."

"Thank you."

"You workin' on somethin' new?"

I nearly fell into the Conway Gibson trap.

"Not at the moment, just keeping my options open …"

Levi eyed me before making his next move.

"You ever been in California?"

"No, can't say I have."

"You oughta give it a try. I knew a few good people out there … producers and such … could put you in touch …"

"I've spoken to Boris Cantini over there. Kenny Rolands, who was my producer on a few things, knows him."

Levi gave me a confiding look.

"I know Boris real well … good friend of mine. He's on Sunset, you should check him out when you come over."

All of a sudden the prospect of a trip to America began to sound enticing. I was doubtless at that point in my life when I was ready to be talked into such a venture.

"Let's keep in contact … we'll sort out some dates. I'd certainly like to give it a try."

"Good thinkin', Jack. Let's do it."

As for *Journey in a Shallow Place*, I wouldn't have said it was the worst movie I had ever started watching, but it was close. If I was forced to give reasons for its awfulness they would have included an abysmal script, bad direction and wooden acting. Why movies with such obvious flaws ever get screened still remains a mystery to me. Maybe the people who make them don't even notice. Was the whole notion of Film School an illusion, or were we all now firmly locked into an entitlement culture? The thinking seemed to be that anyone could be anything they wanted, regardless of whether they had the talent or the aptitude.

A movie can so easily consist of a formulated collection of shots. When the gloss is removed there is very little underneath—neither structure nor organic development. Real ideas or originality are absent, ideas never explored. After twenty minutes of cinematic drivel I could stand it no longer and made for the exit.

Announcing to Jane that I was making a solo trip to the West Coast did not receive a good press. I could have anticipated her reaction, but would still have done anything to avoid a full scale confrontation. Years of life together had not served to mellow either of us; if anything we had hardened our own veneer of individuality. As so often happens, a few glasses of wine at dinner sent any circumspection to the four winds.

"Why are you going to America?"

"To see what I can set up there. I want to make new contacts … see what I can get together."

"Seeing what women you can pick up …"

I was indignant.

"Did I say that?"

"You didn't need to. I've been your convenient fuck for too long, now you want a change."

"I don't think that's true."

"*I do!*"

Jane banged her glass down hard. Fortunately for the tablecloth, it was empty.

"Jack we've been together for ten years … we got engaged once … nothing came of that though did it?"

"I thought maybe …"

She cut in, like a boy racer on a dual carriageway.

"That's what you don't do … *think*! I've been with you … waiting for you …"

Her voice was pleading.

"I kept wondering if there was ever going to be a time when you would actually allow me into your life … or even admit that I existed. Was there? No!"

"I've been working, so have you."

She gave me the laser beam treatment.

"Didn't you ever consider … *once* … in all the time we've been together I might want to have kids?"

She was almost screaming in anger while at the same time her eyes were brimming with tears.

"I'm nearly bloody forty! I want to have my own

children! Is that too much to ask?"

I couldn't look at her; this was the quarrel I had fondly believed I could avoid.

"People get together, have a relationship, then they start a family. That's what happens in real life. You're so obsessed with your bloody *films* you don't know what it is anymore."

I knew whatever I said wouldn't make the slightest difference, but I tried.

"I don't think that's true …"

She shut me up.

"You can't *give* to anybody … you don't know how to anymore. You've forgotten what it's like to be an ordinary human being."

My response was anything but original.

"What do you want me to do?"

"Be kind to me. Treat me properly. *Anyone* would do that better than you do!"

Maybe I was kidding myself I was different, but in her eyes I wasn't.

"I thought I did …"

She looked as if she was about to strike me with one of any number of objects that were nearby.

"You don't know how to behave decently … like a … a … *proper person*. That's because you can get away with doing anything in your bloody movies!"

"But that's different …"

Jane looked at me, accusingly.

"Is it?"

She began to sob, and I knew instinctively her tears were not for herself, or for me. The world was cruel and indifferent, that was the tragedy. Whether

I was selfish or virtuous made little difference to how Jane felt about her part in it. She got up from the table and I could hear her climbing the stairs. There was something terribly final in her movements. I continued to sit and think, debating the situation but getting no nearer the truth. Maybe the answer lay squarely in what I had dedicated my life to doing.

The essence of cinema is the creating of illusion. The artist hones his skills to produce the most convincing fakery. How ruthless he must be to manifest his vision! By following his inspiration, at the cost of spurning convention he is branded as an outlaw. One who lives through the imagination abides by different rules. The philosopher would debate the paradox, why do we value something that is worthless—a photograph, or a painting—and ignore the real treasures within the human heart?

By believing in my own powers it seemed I had unwittingly caused pain to another close to me, something I would not have anticipated. Such a realisation went deep; deeper than I could possibly know at that moment. No matter how far I travelled I could never escape the truth.

13

In the three years that had elapsed since 9/11, the rampant paranoia that had engulfed America had subsided a little. No one could have predicted how the years that followed would affect her spirit. Not that I was familiar with the Land of the Free, apart from what I had gleaned from—guess what—movies. I had spent a weekend in New York for the American premiere of *Billabong*, but that had given me only the merest glimpse. The Hilton, a limo and endless schmoozing in a conference centre, those were the only impressions I took away with me.

Taking a flight to LA seemed like a great adventure. Although only in economy class, the procedure was novel enough to excite me. The sight of the Cascades from 40,000 ft. as we flew south towards California I would never forget. I sampled the meals, drank what was offered to me, and avoided the in-flight entertainment. I read too, mainly a biography of Ronald Pitt. A pioneer of Fifties cinema, he wrote screenplays, some of which were made into movies. When he died, his PC was stolen. The hard drive was found six months later, but nothing could be downloaded from it. What masterpieces might have been lost?

In a diary entry, Pitt offers a warning, one I did not heed at the time or later. He insisted that Hollywood will always dominate the movie industry, likening it to a giant shredder that eats people and ideas.

Late afternoon was when I first saw the City of Angels. The vast urban sprawl had not been exaggerated when people described it, nor the disorientating effect of arriving at LAX. After a surprisingly easy encounter with immigration, I collected my bag from the carousel. There was no one in arrivals to welcome me. No placard with my name on it being held high in the air. Instead I had to battle with the chaos of the concourse and find a cab to take me to the nearest Motel 59. We cut through the yellow and brown banks at each side of Highway 1 until the sea was revealed under a blinding sun—my first sight of Manhattan Beach.

For those who have never experienced the cheapest motel chain in the US, more minimal it is not possible to get. I would imagine sleeping in the OK Corral would be more luxurious. Grateful to see a phone by the bedside, I needed to make plans without delay. I called Ed Levi and left a message saying I would contact him the next day. Boris Cantini I did get to speak to, and we arranged to meet in Long Beach the next morning. I was starting to feel tired, but I was determined to stay with the West Coast rhythm and headed for the beach. Strolling along the Strand, the walkway that ran alongside the shore, I looked out upon the limitless ocean and felt close to paradise.

Before taking a cab to Long Beach the next

morning I talked to Ed. He had arranged for us to meet Avery Biebermann in Glendale that afternoon. The air was blissfully warm when I arrived at *Pratchetts* café. Boris—tanned and smooth in classic West Coast style—greeted me outside.

"Great to see you, Jack. Howja find California?"

"I certainly like what I've seen so far."

Parked in a seat overlooking the main drag, we talked of England and my reasons for visiting the West Coast.

"LA is a kinda small scene, but if you get to know people, you can get established real quick."

"Do you know someone called Biebermann?"

"Sure, I know him, everybody does. What a piece of work that guy is."

"I have to meet him later today."

"Oh, yeah?

"In Glendale."

I could have said 'the planet Pluto' for all the name meant to me.

"He might not show. Biebermann is kinda well known fer doin' that."

Some explanation was needed for Boris.

"Biebermann has been hustling me on and off since the Eighties to get something going over here … a historical series about Davy Crocket, and Daniel Boone mainly."

Boris shook his head knowingly.

"Plenty of hustlers in California, I kin tell yuh."

"I wrote a screenplay a couple of years ago that he got excited about, that's why he kept calling."

Boris' antennae twitched.

"Yeh? What kinda genre was that?"

"Historical … about the Civil War."

"The *American* Civil War?"

"That's right. I called it *Mason Dixon Line*."

Boris paused, I watched him closely.

"Why doncha send that over to me when you get back. I'd like to see it."

He ordered some more coffee.

"So, how is the movie biz in England right now?"

"It can't be that good, or I wouldn't be over here talking to you."

Boris was obviously thinking along different lines.

"I think it's less expensive to make a feature over there …"

"That's if you have one to make …"

I left it at that, and we chewed the fat for a little longer until Ed arrived. On his home turf he was even more of the operator than he was at our first meeting. He and Boris eyed each other like a couple of alley cats. I promised to keep in touch and climbed into Ed's car, congratulating myself for getting in the right side.

"Okay, man, let's get on over to Glendale, see if the man shows."

"I hear there's a chance he may not …"

"Yuh never know in this town what anybody's gonna do. People say different stuff allatime."

I didn't find this very reassuring, but I had no choice except to go along with whatever happened. That was the way most of the time I was in America. The car sped beneath the green guide signs with their shields marking the highway number. Countless palms studded the route to the Starbucks in Glendale. Ed pulled up in the car lot outside. The chain had just begun flexing its commercial muscle and, as I ordered my latte and a blueberry muffin I looked round at the logo swamped décor.

"Is this the heart of America?"

"I sure hope it's not the soul, man."

After a time it was obvious Mr. B would not be showing up. As we drove back to the coast we chatted in a desultory fashion. On the assumption that everyone has a story to tell, I enquired about Ed's background.

"I'm a kid from Lincoln, Nebraska, who came out West. I didn't figure I wanted to go the way my folks did."

"Do you ever go back there at all?

'Nebraska? Not really. Folks there is nice enough if you don't know 'em too well."

When we arrived back at the motel we made plans. Ed was keen on a trip north into Oregon, the main abode of his contacts outside the state.

"I'll pick yuh up at eight tomorrow mornin'. We'll stop someplace fer breakfast, then make it on to Frisco. You can see a few of the sights. It's five hours of nothing man along I 5 afore we get there."

Ed's description of the drive to San Francisco was accurate enough. One big truck looks like the next, so does a Winnebago. Too many strip malls and gas stations clog the edges of the highway and soon the radio station gets tedious. The Interstate may be the quickest way to go from place to place in America, but the big sky stretching into infinity and a few scrubby trees is a bleak outlook. When the way has been carved into the hills, a colour like baked wheat is revealed. Eventually, we took 580 to pass by Oakland and into the city of San Francisco. Ed leaned over in my direction as I was gazing at all around me.

"You better see the Haight. Round fifty years too late, man … but there y'go."

We pushed past the beggars that lined the sidewalk; one was holding up a sign with the legend 'Waiting for a big fat slice'. Ben and Jerry's ice cream seemed a haven from the street until my Strawberry Cheesecake flavour toppled from its cone. I looked on helplessly and they gave me another for free.

"I wish I had my camera, man, yer face …"

The Botanical Gardens in Golden Gate Park were another kind of surprise. We returned to the car and got on to Highway 1. Once over the Golden Gate Bridge we were travelling north.

"You could have seen all round Chinatown … another day maybe …"

The sight of the Pacific breakers and the towering rock stacks on the shore more than made up for this oversight. By nightfall we were somewhere outside Mendocino. We found a lodge in the woods and woke to the sound of coyotes. Back on the road the next day, we drove alongside rivers crashing among silver-grey rocks. Distances grew more immense, the horizon falling back like courtiers at the approach of their king. Mountains loomed above us like giant warriors. Indigo, aquamarine and crimson shimmered all around as water and sky became one. The might of unconquered nature seeped into my blood and filled my mind with awe. At last I had unlocked the key to the secret garden, or at least the hot house.

When we crossed the border into Oregon things were very different. The nearest town—Ashland—was a hip oasis in a redneck county. Ed kept an apartment here in a side street off the main drag. Our first meeting was scheduled for the next day. I hoped Ed had set me up with some useful contacts though I had my doubts. Wave upon wave of ideas was laid on me, but none of them leading to any opportunity for a project. I quickly realised much of what was proposed was only half-considered. On the surface it all seemed enticing— glowing with the energy of the *here and now*. This is the allure of America, the promise of the bigger and better—greater achievement, maximum pleasure. Hit the gas pedal, squeeze as much sensation from each and every moment. By the time I had sat down with the fourth or fifth bunch of people I had almost forgotten what I was trying to achieve. I was exhausted with trying to make not just a telling response, but to say anything that made sense. In between these gatherings I tried to discuss my frustrations with Ed. His response was bizarre.

"Don't believe in yer own mystique, man."

Was that a putdown? A critique that I harboured too many illusions about myself? I would have countered that those I met considered themselves to be major players, but were simply individuals taken up exclusively with their own affairs. Apart from an initial curiosity, they had not the slightest interest in me *or* my ideas.

Caught in this rushing, rolling tide, I could easily sink without trace beneath the waves. What was also bothering me was a distinct feeling that all was not well on the domestic front. Every time I called Jane I got the answer phone, and calls to her newly acquired mobile brought no response either.

When I returned home and opened the front door at Richardson Gardens, I knew things were wrong, very wrong. I rushed upstairs, to see that all Jane's belongings had disappeared.

It took a man of letters—Robert Burton—to profoundly describe depression. *Anatomy of Melancholy* says it all:

And from these melancholy dispositions no man living is free, no Stoick, none so wise, none so happy, none so patient, so generous, so godly, so divine, that can vindicate himself; so well-composed, but more or less, some time or other, he feels the smart of it.

I had become a mad Lear upon the cliff-top wondering whether to throw myself into oblivion and end it all. Once the dark Pit opened before me I could do nothing but circle its treacherous edge. Many times I woke in those terrible nights believing I had fallen into its deeps never to return. Guilt and despair enveloped me and I felt a growing certainty that nothing in my life, or the world about me had any worth. The most insidious aspect of depression is that it appears to offer a cloak of comfort, one the victim cannot willingly surrender. Because the state of darkness has become so familiar, anything beyond its borders seems alien and dangerous—even the light of joy.

Denying my feelings had eventually seared my soul. My emotions had been locked up so tight that they had inevitably broken out to escape into the open. I found myself in some metaphysical space, trying to get away from everything I was experiencing. Yet none of it would go away. How could it? Whatever it was in my head, I was stuck with it. If I thought that I could dispel any mood by taking a long walk, or sitting quietly in silence, I was altogether mistaken.

At the very heart of my pain was the knowledge that I had cruelly neglected Jane. Some nights I would wake and vow to seek her out. Go searching in the night and, when I found my love, promise to cherish her forever. That could never be. I did not know where she was. Jane had made sure of that. The past was not the same land of delight I had known before; regret had usurped my happiness. Karma towered above me, casting its endless shadow. I had to seek help, from those who knew the ways of the endless labyrinth that was the mind.

The river that ran along the outskirts of the city had not been used for traffic since the Middle Ages. Brian Mills, a Jungian psychiatrist, lived in a doughnut-shaped cottage on one of its banks. Arriving promptly for my appointment, I discovered a huge marmalade cat sitting on the doorstep, daring me to enter. Summoning enough courage to ring the doorbell, I was ushered inside where I crawled into the corner of a shiny, leather sofa. To say I was feeling most vulnerable would have been an understatement.

Mills was fleshy and avuncular. A cafetiere was perched on a low table beside him. He spoke in tones of reason, never straying from the path unless he wished to search the mental undergrowth for gems. I was willing to join him on his journey, answering his questions as we jogged along. A man with no opinions makes poor company and I was thankful that he owned a few.

"All these wonderful ideas you have in your movies … where do they come from? Dreams?"

I agreed they might do, though mine hadn't been especially pleasant lately.

"We need you, Jack, you're valuable to us … you enhance our world."

Quicker than I thought the hour session was up. I felt a strange calm, something I had not known for a long time. We smiled at each other profusely, I paid the man and left. As I closed the door, tiptoeing carefully round the feline, I knew something had changed in me. Some power had reached inside my being and impartially examined its essence. Whatever was discovered there had been declared unique and more important—valuable. I had something to offer the world, and thus a reason to continue. I felt like singing, and I did so—loudly—as I drove back to Clinton.

I was kept busy all through that long hot Summer with directing pop videos for *Tumbleweed*, an Anglo-American company. While on the set of the last one filmed I talked to one of the dancers. Christine was tall, dark as night, and had a smile so wide I could lose myself in it. Some years my junior, this didn't seem to bother her. She accepted my invitation to the house, and when she appeared, looked around carefully, taking in everything she saw. In twenty years I had collected not only Victorian furniture but some exotic stuff as well. Christine accepted some tea and kept smiling at me, as she had from the moment she arrived.

"Come round again."

"Yes, I'd like that."

On her next visit I put my arms around her and we kissed in a tentative fashion. She drew back and looked at me with a fixed expression.

"We're not going to have sex, I won't let you."

I said nothing, simply retiring to the sofa. A few moments later Christine had obviously changed her mind. She was standing in front of me, completely naked. I couldn't get my clothes off fast enough. They say sex and courage are entwined, and I could feel my spirits rise at the same rate as my libido. Christine and I began to see each other regularly and her presence renewed my interest in movies and everything else in my life.

Convinced that a production company in America was the way ahead, I called Boris and we set up *Butternut Productions* in LA. The next step was for me to write a screenplay for a future project. That now seemed a daunting task; I was so much in the groove of being a director that I was stuck there. The big change was going to be making myself think like an artist. I had got so used to implementing other people's ideas that I had none of my own.

There was no difficulty for me inventing scenes to film, but I was determined to avoid assembly line methods of movie making. How places and people related to each other was the magic that made any good story. Mega-budget, star-filled epics, when they fail, do so because they have no heart. When people like your film work they do so because they like *you*. Your audience is grateful to the person who made something special happen for them.

Wrestling with my creative daemon during the day was very different from my nights. I was held aloft by the lightness of love for Christine and, I assumed, her love for me. A hint of melancholy accompanied our passion, as if we both knew it could not last. True love can never be anything else except a feeling of completeness. When Christine was not there and I thought about her, my feelings almost overwhelmed me.

One of the cardinal rules for a film-maker is to never to personally finance any project. That said, raising funds in the twenty-first century in England was almost impossible, we were now a third-world country. I looked back fondly to the days when Douglas—now the Earl of Mahogany—would willingly distribute largesse.

Desperate times called for desperate measures and I found myself contacting Dave Whitefield, a move I would never have entertained before. We arranged to meet at *Quatro's* in Clinton. From the moment he arrived at this semi-swanky venue I knew this was going to be awkward, and I was right. Whitefield rose to shake hands with me and, as he did so, I was on my guard. I had noticed a dull glint in his eyes, something I did not like. I ordered a latte and started on my pitch.

I had not got very far in when Whitefield interrupted.

"I hope you've got a decent part for Mandy in all this …"

"Who's Mandy?"

He muttered almost inaudibly.

"My girlfriend."

This was interesting news, I had always considered him a married man.

"Anyway, you owe me, sunshine …"

"For what?"

"Letting me down … and Mandy …"

I stared uncomprehending.

"She should have been in that fucking movie!"

"What movie? What are you on about?

"You been to America aintcha? I know you have … talking to people in Hollywood …"

"I've been to *California* … that doesn't mean …"

The dull glint was gone, his eyes lit up like plastic coach lamps.

"Fixing up a movie … *without getting Mandy sorted* … while you were doing it."

I wondered if he and I were on the same planet.

"I didn't fix up any movie when I was there … I wish I had."

"I oughta take you apart!"

I backed away.

"Have you gone mad?"

"If that means angry … yeah I am … very angry."

I shook my head.

"I don't believe any of this."

Throwing a fiver on the table, I got up to leave.

"Here … my treat …"

I was still stunned when I walked back to the house. Once or twice I looked around to see if Whitefield, or some hit man he had hired, was following me. I called Pete and, rather breathlessly, told my tale. As always, his demeanour was as the proverbial mill pond.

"Don't worry about it, mate. He's been doing that to everyone lately … he's on one … totally lost it."

"Who's this Mandy?"

Pete tsked and tutted.

"You know how old she is? *Fifteen.*"

I didn't think I wanted to hear any more.

"He promised her parents he'd make their little daughter a star … they must be more loopy than he is."

"I seriously thought of getting the law in, the way he was carrying on to me."

"Nah … he's all mouth and no trousers. You know what his nickname always was?"

"No."

"*Yapper.*"

I left it at that, and went off to think about matters more conducive.

15

Two weeks later I got a call from Kenny, cutting to the chase straightaway, as always.

"So what's happening with you?"

I sighed. I had to.

"Trying to get people to give me money mainly."

Kenny spied the sub-plot immediately.

"So which of these endless projects of yours are you trying to get finance for, Mr. Director?"

I protested, mildly.

"Hang on! Just one … of my novel."

"Remind me …"

"*My movie of Paper Sun.*"

"Oh, that. The one nobody wants to make …"

I ignored the barb.

"Somebody might. In America … *not here*. That's bloody obvious."

Kenny relented—a little.

"I'm sorry … I shouldn't try to curb your boundless optimism."

"The charming Englishman abroad still has some advantage …"

Kenny returned to the fray.

"Doesn't matter how much charm you have, what counts is having the cheque in the bank."

I kept my counsel.

"You're going to America again?"

"I think so, to follow up the historical movie."

"Not given up on that one either yet then?"

"One of the film boards I contacted some time ago is still interested … and there are still potential investors."

"*Potential*? What does that mean?"

"Okay, I hear you … but if I can make *that* movie, then I can finance my own."

Kenny whistled, tunelessly.

"And how many times have I heard that? If only X will happen then I can do Z …"

"*Tread softly for you tread on my dreams.*"

"Some dreams need treading on … so they can be put out of their misery."

"*Touché.*"

"I'm just an old cynic, don't mind me."

I paused.

"Be good get some work to pay for the trip too … something might turn up, I suppose."

Kenny sniffed loudly.

"So will Christmas."

It was overdue for me to ask what she was up to.

"I really do want to go to Japan for an *Anime* conference, but I'm supposed to go to LA myself sometime. Problem is I don't know when …"

I thought how good it would be to make a film with Kenny at the helm, conveniently forgetting the old adage that one should be careful what one wishes for.

* * *

Christine had moved into Richardson Gardens and I was definitely not complaining. Endless passion is addictive. After her part as a dancer in the video, no other work came in for her. She was forced to take some mundane job and, as she never talked about it, I didn't either. When we were sitting around together Christine would not take her eyes off me. I wondered if she was reassuring herself that I actually existed. It was impossible to tell. She often acted as if she owned a monopoly on emotion and was the only one who knew how anyone else felt.

I continued to struggle with the screenplay, having decided to go for what I had told Kenny, adapting *Paper Sun*. Being an artist is a disadvantage in a relationship, dreams being more intense than reality. No one likes to be second best, especially involving a rival that only exists in their lover's imagination. Away from matters of the heart, I had to consider the changes that were happening in the biz. These were radical.

Before, filming had been an exclusive, expensive, and often wasteful process. Equipment was cumbersome, and a hierarchical structure was needed on any production. With the advent of HD video it was now possible for the independent moviemaker to be director, cinematographer, soundman, and editor. Because everything is lightweight and portable, digital technology makes old-style film equipment resemble a vintage railway engine. Maintaining and placating this monster was one of the reasons Hollywood became synonymous with escalating and unreal costs.

The other side of the coin was that the limitless

possibilities of the new media had made form triumph over content. With digital colour correction, every interior was blue and everyone had a Manhattan Beach tan. Teal and orange won the day every time. Digital images could be manipulated too, rather like bad notes being excised in a recording studio. When the human element becomes subordinate to technology, the quality of ideas suffers. Art should be an expanding of thought not a limitation. What I did not know was that I was about become involved with a project that comprehensively demonstrated the pitfalls I have just described.

Christine had just left for work when my phone buzzed. I reached over from the pillows and grabbed it. Pete's voice sounded in my ear.

"Listen, I only just heard about this from Kenny. She was rushing off to the airport …"

"As she does …"

"Yeah, all that flying … it might be easier if she grew some wings."

"So what great tidings did she have to impart?"

"She wanted to tell you there's a job going as a *creative consultant.*"

I did a double-take, one Pete obviously couldn't see.

"What's that when it's at home?"

"Just means you're on set telling people about things they don't know about. Plenty of guys making films these days who haven't got a clue what they're doing."

"There probably always were, we just didn't realise

it. Got a number?"

"I can text it across ... guy called Barry Miller is the director."

"Great, thanks."

"You never know, night work out. Give him a call."

I assured Pete I would do so.

16

When I told Christine I was going to be working on a movie she seemed enthusiastic. Sometimes it was difficult to know what she really thought about anything. Like a lot of people, she associated moviemaking with the glamorous life. I knew the reality was very different. Although my conversation with Barry Miller had been relaxed, he sounded very young. I detected a whiff of the hassles that had plagued *Stilton*. Even so, I had agreed to take the job.

I had yet to see a copy of the screenplay, though I did know the movie was titled *Circus Waltz*. When I finally got to see Barry's script it was too late anyway. We were to begin shooting in the middle of January, the first location being *Hugh's Bar* in Clinton. When I arrived at the location early in the morning there was no sign of the kind of activity I would usually associate with the first day on a set. No vehicles or personnel were anywhere, least of all a director. I called Barry. The voice that answered sounded like someone who had woken from a deep sleep.

"Barry?"

"Yeah … who's this?

"This is Jack. I'm here at the location."

"Oh, yeah, right. What time did I say?"

"You told me to get there at eight."

"Did I? I don't think anyone's going to be around until a bit later. Can you go and get yourself a cup of coffee or something?"

"If no one's here in an hour I'll give you another call."

Barry's voice sounded as if it came from inside his pillow.

"Okay, thanks. Sorry about all this."

When I returned, there was still nothing going on. I couldn't see the point of calling again, and as my car was parked within sight of the entrance, I could easily see when anyone appeared. At half-past ten a Fiat Uno parked in front of me. Several tousled-looking figures emerged from it—three youths and a girl—all looking as if they had just come straight from a party. I identified the director from his photograph on the movie's website, and got out of my car.

"Hello."

Barry spun round, his features registering surprise and terror in equal measure.

"Hi! Are you Jack?"

Close up, Barry looked about seventeen, those with him about the same age. Before I had time to say anything further, another car pulled up behind Barry's vehicle. The window zipped down.

"Where the fuck have you been? Is your phone switched off?"

Barry attempted cool.

"Toby, when I'm driving I always …"

One of the girls was peering through the window

of *Hugh's Bar*. She turned towards Barry.

"There's nobody in there. Are you sure they know we're coming?"

Before Barry could reply Toby started yelling again.

"Not more fuck ups? Can't you get anything right?"

Barry was desperately fiddling with his phone, while the girls tapped on the windows. Two other cars had arrived disgorging floppy-haired types and more girls.

"Hi. Hi. Listen … we can't get in and …"

Some of the new arrivals clustered around the entrance to the bar, others remained on the pavement. None of them seem to know what was going on, or were the slightest concerned with Barry's plight.

"Yeah, I arranged that someone would be here to let us in a bit before ten … I'm the guy who's doing the movie."

I chatted briefly to Toby, who I had not seen since we worked on *Billabong* together. He looked older and more cynical. Barry came over and joined us.

"Not my fault … not my fault at all. Somebody didn't look at their texts … telling them to be here and letting us in."

Eventually, we got inside the bar and some semblance of organisation took place, but not much. The girls flitted about stroking their touch screens. Occasionally one of them would be called into make-up. It was now nearly noon. I returned to Toby.

"Much on?"

Sharp was the response.

"Not really, else I wouldn't be doing something like this would I?"

Realising our cameraman was not in the best of tempers, I left it at that. Elsewhere, a corner of the bar was being lit, presumably for the first set-up. I wandered outside, nobody seeming to notice. When I came back I went to confirm financial arrangements with Barry. We sat at one the tables near the bar.

"You'd like to be paid at the end of each week, I expect."

"That would be handy."

"I'll have a cheque for you on Friday."

There was an awkward pause. Barry fiddled with his phone, turning it this way and that while occasionally glancing at the screen. He was obviously thinking he ought to give me some account of what he was intending to do next.

"We're just getting the first scene sorted out. I'll rehearse everybody in a minute."

"You haven't done the blocking?"

A perfectly ordinary enquiry, but Barry took it amiss.

"I had some other *really important* things to do."

He glared at me as he said this, and went off clutching his phone. It was now two o' clock.

The next day I again studiously arrived at 8 a.m. but I need not have bothered. No actual filming got started until way past noon. As the previous day, no one—aside from Toby—seemed to know what was going on at all. From out of this directorial mire emerged the first set up of the day, two actors at the bar talking.

They rehearsed without Barry, as he was involved in a whispered conversation with one of the girls. His features had assumed a deep red and I suspected he had either asked for a date, or had been turned down.

Eventually shooting began, being abandoned several times by the sound man holding the boom at the wrong angle, or adjustments having to be made to the lighting. Once more Barry had neglected to do any blocking and, as soon as the actors moved away from the bar, they were in total darkness. The background actors had been given no direction, and were either too prominent or off camera.

For someone who had actually directed a successful feature or two, this was all a touch galling. I was deliberately not going to interfere, just wait until I was approached for advice, if needed. When this did happen it always involved something trivial. As the week wore on I began to feel more and more redundant. To stop getting terminally bored I decided to offer my views about what was going on rather than wait to be asked.

When I did so, it was clear Barry resented any suggestion I might make. I found his attitude not only arrogant, but bizarre. Here was some young kid who knew nothing about movies trying to give everyone, including me, the impression he was a veteran. I was reduced to a state that hovered between frustration and downright amazement. The slipshod way everything was done was beyond belief. The boom op. would be texting during takes, oblivious to the mike swinging into shot. I was certain the sound man was barely competent, and the actors seemed totally bored. Whenever he caught my eye, the cameraman would shake his head, eyes skyward.

I was not wholly surprised when Toby asked me for a contact number at the end of the day. He obviously had something to impart. The call came as I was preparing dinner for Christine and myself. The meal was at the stage where I could leave it to look after itself in the oven.

"Hi, hope you don't mind me calling …"

Here was a scenario probably repeated *ad infinitum* all over the world after a day's filming. The director complains about the producer, or the crew, or vice-versa. On this occasion it was the cameraman cussing the director. Toby didn't pull his punches when describing Barry's shortcomings.

"I don't know what you think, but I reckon he's a total tosser."

"He's young …"

"I wouldn't mind if he knew what he was doing for about half a minute, at any time during the day."

"He certainly doesn't give the impression of being in control …"

"Which makes it twice as hard for me, because he doesn't know what kind of shot he wants … *or* how he wants anything lit. So, it ends up with me making all the decisions, *and* telling everyone else what to do."

I sympathised as best I could.

"Yeah, it must be a bit soul-destroying for you."

Toby launched into his spiel.

"Before we started, I told him to mug up on the techniques of filmmaking and the director's role on the set, even the *basics*. He obviously hasn't done any homework at all."

I asked the obvious question.

"Has he ever directed anything before, do you know?"

"I don't think so. Basically, it's you and me who know what we're doing, and that's all. The rest of it is just his friends trying to get something together. He sets a dreadful example too … he's the worst one for messing around."

"Where's the funding coming from?"

"I heard he's got a rich uncle …"

This was not a euphemism, apparently. Barry's father had several brothers 'in the city', thus money was no object. It seemed I had once more been drawn into a vanity project, as the bee to the sticky stuff. Toby was obviously on edge.

"Tell me honestly, do you think this is going to happen?"

"Get done, you mean? Shot and edited?"

"Yeah, an actual movie coming out of it."

I tried to be ever hopeful; it was a habit hard to lose after forty years.

"I would have thought it was just possible."

"Miracles might happen and Barry gets himself together?"

I had to distance myself a little from all this or I was being a total hypocrite. After all, the guy was paying me.

"It's not a situation I've ever been familiar with. You remember what *Billabong* was like … all those years ago … we all worked bloody hard."

I could tell this didn't satisfy Toby. He obviously

wanted me to take his side against Barry, something I wasn't prepared to do. He resorted to being waspish.

"You know why he got you in don't you?"

"Tell me."

"So he could say to his uncle that he'd got a famous filmmaker involved … he could go around showing off to his friends that you were part of his movie."

"That doesn't really bother me, Toby … he can say what he wants."

"It's all a total fantasy … complete bollocks …"

I heard the sound of the key in the lock, and Christine's voice.

"That's my girlfriend, I'd better go."

"Really? Okay. See you on the set tomorrow."

I was sure from Toby's incredulous tone he considered I was far too old for any kind of liaison.

On Week 2 there were even more extraneous people hanging around on the set. Who they were, or what they were doing there I never discovered. Barry reacted in his usual schizophrenic way; playing up to the crowd one minute then getting temperamental if a take was interrupted.

Time spent shooting was at a premium. On several occasions Barry did the last take at 4 p.m. and, as we had not started till nearly 11 a.m., this made for a very short day. I dutifully stuck to my hours, arriving at 8 a.m. and leaving at 6 p.m.. Breaking the contract was a risk I would not take, even though Barry might display a total licence.

On Friday, after handing me a cheque, he invited me out to lunch.

"Meet me at my place tomorrow ... don't worry ... I'll pay."

"Thank you very much."

Barry giggled nervously. I sensed that, like Toby, he was keen to confide in me.

"I'm in Upper Clinton ... Sandy Down Rd ... No. 6 ... it's got a sort of double balcony. Around twelve?"

Barry took me to an up-market restaurant called *Dorian*, heavy on the chromium, and with more windows than wall space. It was hardly my style, but it did prove there *was* such a thing as a free lunch. Barry was obviously no stranger to the place, adopting a patrician air from the off. I waited patiently while he informed the staff he wanted his regular table and such like. We ordered steak and drank *Enrique*, some expensive lager I'd never heard of. The purpose of the occasion quickly became clear. After a few *non-sequiturs* about how well he thought the movie was going, Barry began to complain about Toby.

"I had a text from him this morning. Ridiculous! You wouldn't believe it ... he wants to reshoot all of yesterday's stuff because the lighting wasn't right ..."

I was even.

"You changed it though. Half-way through, re-member?"

Barry sipped his lager.

"I know I did ... it had to be like that."

"It did?"

"The ambiance wasn't right if we didn't have it my way."

I gently attempted reason.

"The problem is, those fill lights you're using

aren't really up to the job. It's very dark in that bar … and I'm not sure that's a 4K set up Toby's using either, for some reason. You should check that."

I didn't think this was going in, but pressed on.

"If he uses a sensor lens that'll help with the light … and the contrast …"

"You sound very knowledgeable …"

This was definitely a tad patronising, but I was equal to it.

"You've got to know what's technically possible as a director. These days … with digital … unless the monitor is programmed to link with what's on camera you don't get a true image."

Barry applied himself to sawing at his steak.

"Bloody annoying though … Toby wanting to do that all again."

"Probably pissed him off quite a bit too, when he looked at what had been shot."

Barry looked up.

"I'm not sure I can get the bar any more as a location."

I remembered my role as consultant.

"When you're planning a shoot, it's always best to assume that things will take longer than you think."

"Problem is … it's all down to me …"

"Yeah, you could have certainly done with a producer … or a line producer at least. Someone to organise things …"

Barry looked tetchy.

"The budget won't stretch that far … most of the people working on the movie have volunteered to come along for nothing."

"Having the director's job is quite enough."

I was trying desperately not to sound like I was giving a lecture.

"I know it is! With Toby there, everything seems so much more difficult ..."

I finished my beer and wondered how often people blamed someone else for their own shortcomings. I was also aware the budget for *Circus* could not possibly hold up much longer, or the 'rich uncle' would be bankrupt. I was being paid £500 a day for doing very little, and that was only part of the ever-increasing expenditure.

Sure enough, at the end of Week 6 Barry approached me rather shamefacedly and explained that my tenure was over. I took this calmly enough, pocketed my final cheque and wished him well, along with everyone else on the set. I was now more than ever determined to get my own projects going, although at what cost to my well-being I had not yet realised.

Inexplicably, telling Christine I was no longer in-volved with the movie made her impatient, if not aloof. We had just finished a pizza, one of those delivered to the door along with a free bottle of wine. Neither was particularly satisfying which may have added to the general angst. Christine pushed her plate away brusquely. She was not looking at me either.

"I don't know why you did that ..."

"They couldn't afford to pay me anymore."

"You said most of them were working for nothing. You could have done that too."

"I could have done, but I wasn't prepared to."

She still wasn't looking at me and I could feel her anger.

"This movie might be really good when it's finished."

"I don't think so."

She did look at me then, with an incredulous expression.

"How can you be so sure of that?"

"Because the script's terrible … Barry's directing is non-existent … the crew don't know what they're doing … it's a disaster."

Christine wasn't listening.

"It sounds like he's just a young guy having fun with his friends …"

"I'm sure you're right … but why don't they just go down the pub instead."

Christine smoothed down her skirt in a deliberate way.

"Why do you always have to be so *serious* about everything?"

"I don't like to see time and money wasted. And also filmmaking is my job …"

"I have a job, but I don't really care about it."

This was the first time Christine had ever mentioned work.

"That's a shame."

"Is it? There's hundreds … thousands probably of people just like me … all doing something they don't really want to do, every day."

Her expression changed and she began to look resentful.

"I don't think you even notice other people exist …"

I took this calmly enough, but could sense danger.

"I noticed you."

"Only because I was dancing … I was a performer … so I was part of your little world."

"I would have been interested in you wherever I met you."

Christine looked at me even more impatiently. We sat in silence. It went on for too long. Neither of us was capable of reaching out to the other.

Boris Cantini was his usual sunny self when I called him. California probably did that to people.

"How are you, my friend? Good to hear from you."

"I'm thinking of coming over …"

"To California?"

"No … Kentucky."

I could imagine his amused look.

"Okay. Any real reason? You like Bluegrass? Bourbon?"

"To try and get funding for the Civil War movie."

"Has Biebermann come back on that?"

"Not really, you know what *he's* like …"

"Yeh, kinda flaky …"

"Is *Butternut* still registered over there?"

"Sure is … and the checking account."

"At least I'll have somewhere to put the money if and when I get it."

I braced myself for the pitch.

"I was wondering if …"

In that boundless American way, Boris was ready for anything.

"What do you need from me, my friend?"

"Somewhere to stay for a week or so. I don't think I can handle those Motel 59 places anymore."

"Yeh, I know what you mean. I have some very good friends who are in New Albany. You fly into Louisville when you come in, right?"

"I think so … I haven't booked the flight yet."

"New Albany is just over the border in Indiana. I'm sure I can get these guys to pick you up from the airport."

"That would be amazing."

"Okay, I'm on it. They're Marcie and Bobby Pinkerton; the family owned a big farm round that way somewhere once, in Harrison County maybe."

"Thanks, Boris."

"No worries. Catch you later."

I had an image of cattle and cowboy hats which quickly faded after I clicked off the phone. Christine had announced she had to stay late at work. This gave me a chance to book the flight and compile some sort of itinerary. Her absence made me reflect on how little I really knew her. When one veil was lifted it always revealed another, so I could never discover the real person beneath.

17

My decision to fly to Louisville didn't go down well with Christine. This was a rerun of the hassle I had with Jane ten years before. She stared at me, her eyes cold and accusing.

"I'm going now."

Within minutes she had gathered her few possessions and was going towards the door. She stood in the street for a moment then turned and began to walk away. I continued to stare into the night for a time then got in my car and followed her. By the time I reached her flat she was already inside, the light was on. I rang the bell and after an interval she opened the door. When I went to put my arms around her she drew back. She did not stop me, however, when I followed her into the small flat. I took the one chair in the room while Christine sat on the corner of the bed. She would still not look at me.

"Why are you so difficult?"

"Am I?"

She turned her head, sweeping away my words.

"I don't want to see you ever again."

I tried to breathe. It wasn't easy.

"I don't love you anymore, so there's not much point is there?"

"No …"

My apparent calm seemed to inflame her.

"Why can't you see? Why can't you see *anything*?"

It was impossible to remain in the room. Christine was counting the steps until I reached the door. I paused to say goodbye. She did not answer.

I flew into Louisville two days later, at the end of March. The stopover in Detroit gave me the opportunity to take a nap, but this didn't happen. Far too wired up by the prospect of being in America again, and trying to raise funds for a movie that had been hanging around for perhaps too long, I couldn't relax. I was also still bruised by the break up with Christine—a strange mixture of the valiant and the vulnerable. Gradually, the whole episode was to assume such an ethereal quality that it drifted away like the early morning mist.

Concourse A seemed to stretch for miles, but when I finally got to the exit and the carousel to pick up my bag, I was given a tickertape welcome. What looked like the entire Pinkerton family and every one of their cousins had gathered to welcome me to Kentucky. Marcie advanced with open arms while the man of the piece hovered in her wake, smiling like a Belisha beacon.

"Hi, I'm Marcie, and this is my husband Bobby."

I shook hands with everyone, even the myriad of children that were clustered about.

"And that's Cyndi, Randy, Mark, Kaye, Ron, Cathy, Janice, Jamie and George-Ann. Bobby and me, we both been married before … you kinda collect 'em on the way, y'know."

And off we went, with every soul in the truck looking wide-eyed at the strange visitor from afar. I wondered if I was expected to pass out trinkets or beads to the natives—gifts from afar. We drove beside the glistening Ohio and, with the river left behind, the Indiana country closed in around us. A land of pine woods, spreading elms and cattle, it perfectly reflected the Pinkertons and their Southern ways.

The next day, without a murmur, Marcie drove the fifty miles to the state capital so I could attend my meeting. She even arranged to go shopping while I spent an hour ensconced with the movie dignitaries, arranging to see me later. On the way, Highway 64 offered little that was new. Billboards, strip malls, and gas stations came and went with a dull regularity.

The State Film Board had their suite of offices in a Tower of Babel in the centre of the city. I had not dressed up for the occasion and felt like a hillbilly at a Southern Ball. Business was slow, mainly because it was all too clear I had come with a screenplay, a begging bowl and little else. The conversation soon became more and more elliptical. The lunch of ham and pickles that was provided was impossible to consume at low volume. I was obliged to babble about England to muffle the scrunching of giant dills.

Marilyn Rook was a sweet soul but obviously nonplussed as to why I should travel several thousand miles with so little prospect of any gain. Buddy Franks, a tall, imposing figure who could, without a hint of comedy, have played a US Marshall, also eyed me with some curiosity. That I had a track record and also, that I was a novelty, alleviated the situation a little.

"I have one or two contacts in New York who might be interested in yer project … I can ask them to give you a call."

"Thank you. Boris Cantini would make an excellent producer, think."

"Boris is such a fine gentleman …"

Marilyn toyed with a cube of Pepperjack cheese before pushing it to the side of her plate.

"The problem is they all want stars these days. Y'know we had one hundred and fifty-six proposals to film here last year, an' I think only just a few of them actually ever got started."

Franks didn't seem to want to be left out of any action if it was happening.

"No reason why we just can't look at a coupla likely places you might wanna use for locations in yer movie, Mr. Strange. I'd be happy to show you around."

The next day was spent pleasantly enough, investigating mansions, tobacco barns, and a jailhouse. We even took in a tour of a distillery and sniffed the vats of fermenting liquor. Franks had organised lunch with the mayor of a town that was, I was informed, celebrated for the crafting of brooms. The speciality of the house was chicken and dumplings with turnip greens and black-eyed peas, a delicacy I had never encountered. Present at the lunch were a posse of would-be investors in my movie. They were polite but, like the genial Ms. Rook, slightly puzzled as to my mission. For some reason I could not understand, conversation mainly revolved around food.

"Y'all have fried pies back there in England, Mr. Strange? These kinda pies?"

"How about grits?"

"Corn bread? Red eye gravy?"

Afterwards, I wondered if I should have implied that these Southern delicacies were intrinsically a part of Anglo-Saxon culture. Perhaps if I had, Mr. James Reed and Mr. Frank Steiner, among others, might have produced their cheque books with an inordinate flourish. It was, however, not to be. Their billfolds remained firmly ensconced in the vest pockets of their well-tailored coats.

A visit later in the day to a man who was utterly convinced he was Col. John Hunt Morgan, the renowned Confederate hero, had the effect of sending me into the utmost despondency. I realised all of a sudden that wallowing in the history of Gettysburg and the career of Ulysses Grant was not for me. My enthusiasm for the whole project suddenly evaporated.

When I returned to the Pinkertons abode, my mood must have been obvious to Marcie. Over dinner she encouraged me to talk about matters other than those I had been discussing all day. I was only too glad to. The Secession of the Confederacy forgotten, I rather let myself go concerning my aspirations for the kind of film I really wanted to make. While I paused for breath she smiled, with great sympathy and simplicity, I thought.

"Well, I have a surprise for you, Jack. My good friend Dolly … who I spoke with today about you … she really wants to meet up. She's all into the movies and that kinda hokum. Why don't you give her a call?"

After dinner Marcie passed me the phone. One of those Southern Belle accents, that at first I thought was put on for my benefit, came on the line.

"Wal … hello, there."

I introduced myself and briefly explained my mission. Dolly seemed more than enthusiastic.

"That sounds so interesting … so why don't you just drop by and have dinner tomorrow night?

"Thank you, I will. That's very kind."

"Oh, that's no problem, sweetie pie. Marcie will bring you right to my little home. I sure do hope you like it."

I suddenly felt inspired once more, as if by some elusive Cajun magic.

Even before the house came fully into view, the circular drive gave a hint of the medium-range glamour that awaited me. Once inside the front door, the whole panoply of Southern charm was revealed, the centre of it all being Dolly Thorne herself. Resplendent in white, with a shawl thrown casually across her bare shoulders, every lock of her blonde tresses could have been arranged by a portraitist. She held her head to one side, the better for me to catch the sparkle of turquoise in her eyes. My host grasped both of my hands as if she would never let go and stared at me. Her gaze was approaching the range of predatory.

"Oh, this is so wonderful, that you have honoured my home by coming here … an Englishman …"

I was slightly overwhelmed by the eulogy, but did my best to return the compliment.

"My pleasure …"

Dolly was standing much closer to me than was absolutely necessary, her gaping cleavage impossible to ignore. I thought it politic to move away, towards the door of the sitting room. There, overstuffed armchairs, and tables with showily carved legs dominated the scene. Equestrian paintings were arranged on the walls, and clusters of pale globes hung down from the ceiling.

"My daddy just loved to ride … so do I …"

The innuendo was hardly well-disguised, but I did not respond. I chose instead to inspect the titles filling a bookcase near to me. To my surprise there was a copy of *Paper Sun*. Without thinking I reached down and took it from the shelf.

"Excuse me, can I just …"

Dolly seemed pleased that she could be of service.

"Of course, anything you want …"

My novel had fared better in America than at home and, not long after its publication, I began to receive fan mail from Colorado, Oregon, and the Southern states. With a suitably garish 1990s design featuring Spice Girls clones, there it was. Dolly came over, looked at the cover, put two and two together and made a dozen or more.

"Scary biscuits! Yer a famous writer as well as a movie man! Fer gosh sakes! To think the very guy who wrote this here book *is right in my house* …"

Her voice shot up at least half an octave.

"… and I gonna be eatin' dinner with him later!"

She clapped her hands in ecstasy, the full octave being reached.

"I gotta tell you, Mr. Strange, I have loved that book from the day I bought it ... over at the bookstore."

In a bid to prevent any further siren sounds I quickly interjected a platitude.

"I'm so glad you liked it."

"Liked it? Oh, I'm tellin' yuh. That story has been my whole life! I musta read it a dozen times or more."

I boldly aired my plans.

"I'd like to make a film of it ... maybe change some parts ..."

"Well sure, you could do that. Yer clever ... you could do anything ..."

Dolly slipped her arm through mine.

"Why don't we go have dinner and you can tell me all about yer wonderful ideas."

"I'd like to do that."

"Cool beans!"

"Is that what we're having?"

She slapped my arm playfully.

"Oh, yer a hoot! You silly goose!"

Dolly led me across the hall towards the dining room. Here, a more formal décor greeted the visitor— flocked wallpaper, and velvet drapes at the windows. The surface of the dining table was so highly polished it reflected the wine glasses upon it. Dolly sat down at the head of this with me beside her. I had yet to enquire, but there seemed to be no sign of any *Mr. Thorne*.

"Isn't this all so great? Don't you just love this silverware right here?"

I stared at the candlesticks for want of anything better to do. Making remarks about one's surroundings, whether to praise or not, was considered bad form in England. People just got on with things, particularly eating and drinking. Not that I was that much *au fait* with polite society, an invitation to Mahogany House never having been forthcoming.

"And yer over here tryin' to raise money fer yer new movie ... the one of the book?"

I decided to keep it all simple.

"I have a production company over here ... in Louisville ... Butternut Films."

There was an interval while we tucked into the steak and sweet potatoes.

"Wal, I'll tell you this, Mister Strange, I sure as hell do know everybody round here and all over. If anybody can get you what you want it's Dolly Thorne."

In the bright candlelight her eyes sparkled like a zillion diamonds, and just for that moment I believed her.

"Ah."

Dolly kept on sparkling.

"So, what are yer plans fer over here right now?"

"I have one more meeting with some people, then I fly out."

She pouted magnificently.

"That is *such a shame* ... we could really have got to know each other ... really well."

This was undeniably a red-light moment, but I kept my cool.

"You know you are such a good-looking man, I can hardly take my eyes off you."

"Be my guest ..."

I was certain Dolly took this as an invitation for

more than just looking, but I wasn't sure. She kept on gazing.

"An' y'know I just love yer accent … I could go on listening to that forever. My hillbilly heart jes' turned over when you called."

No response, no matter how gallant, would have ever been adequate.

"Talk to me some more …"

I went into some detail about my movie plans, Dolly seeming genuinely interested.

"I think we can get this money for you. I just know I can, and I'm going to work on this real hard."

"Thanks."

"When I have those powerful feelings inside I know I'm never wrong."

The pumpkin pie had come and gone and we still lingered at the table. The wine had made me suitably mellow.

"What are you thinking about, you gorgeous man?"

Before I had time to conjure up any response, Dolly jumped up looking eager.

"I have never showed you the rest of my house! How rude can somebody get!"

I dutifully followed her up the stairs. The absence of a husband still disconcerted me, as signs of domesticity were unmistakeably evident. Would an enraged spouse, concealed in one of the cupboards on the landing, suddenly fly out with a shotgun? I could have protested that all was wholly innocent, but it would have needed a brace of Perry Masons to get me off the hook. We arrived at the bedroom in double-quick time.

"Why don't you go ahead an' read me a bedtime story, lover?"

Dolly was up close again, this time even more so. Quite how we started kissing I wasn't sure. She was purring into my chest.

"Yer so beautiful ..."

She started unbuttoning my shirt with deft fingers.

"Dolly, I'm not sure this is a good idea ..."

Where her hands had now strayed told me she thought it was.

"I do, honey ..."

I thought it time to introduce a reality check.

"Your husband ..."

"Oh, he won't mind, he likes me to have fun ... and boy, am I gonna do that right now ..."

Dolly unzipped my fly and there, proudly revealed, was the root of my being.

"Honey, now that is just *so gorgeous*."

Her mouth was now involved in getting acquainted with her new friend. In no time at all, I let myself go—in more ways than one.

18

England. *Summer 2014.* When I got into the house, dragging my bag, I checked my phone. Linda had called several times. I flipped onto her contact number and waited while I got diverted to message. Calling Kenny came next.

"Hi. You been somewhere?"

"America. Just got back today."

"Trying to get funding for the Civil War thing … anything happen?"

"I may have got funding for my movie …"

Kenny, like Dolly so recently, wasted no time in getting to the point.

"How much?"

"Fifty."

"When can I see the screenplay?"

I hesitated.

"It needs a bit of work first …"

If we had been on Skype I would have seen Kenny jump at the camera.

"*You sold your movie in the US without a script*?"

"They know my book and my movies … so they're going for it on that … *I think*."

"Okay, I'm still listening …"

"I'm just waiting for the go ahead."

"I go to Japan in the next few days … keep me posted with what's going on."

I ate a micro-waved something or other, downed a glass of wine and went to bed. Unpacking could wait until the morning.

Towards the end of the week the jet lag had abated somewhat and I was feeling marginally more human. Linda had not called, but someone else did early on Friday morning. Too early.

"Hey, Jack!

"Dolly!

"What time is it with you there?"

"Around five-thirty …"

"In the morning? Oh, pooperoo. I'm so sorry."

"S'okay, I'm awake now anyway."

"I got real good news for us … I got the funding, all of it from the one guy …"

If I had not been awake before, I was now.

"…Cole Wertheim. He just said okay right there."

"That's amazing!"

"I just said what a great English director you were … that 'Billabong' was one of my favourite movies … and yer book was fantastic too."

A small, dark cloud appeared.

"But he hasn't seen a script …"

"He was dead cool about that … I'd said you'd get that to me whenever."

"ASAP."

"Cole is a crazy old whack ass … but real loaded. Fifty million is nothing to these people … you better believe it. Later!"

I had no choice but to believe it. As it would turn out, there were a lot of things I didn't know about. They were all waiting to jump out and surprise me later.

In the meanwhile, I waited anxiously to call the *Bank of America* when it opened at 3 p.m. our time. After I had gone through all the security checks with the teller he confirmed there was indeed a deposit of fifty million dollars in the *Butternut* account. No one could have stopped me from dancing an impromptu jig up and down the stairs.

Wanting to share the good news I called Linda at work. She wasn't at her desk. Whoever it was answered the phone told me she was on holiday. Slightly baffled by that revelation, I went ahead and called Kenny. I couldn't reach her either. Drinking champagne solo didn't appeal too much, so I continued working on the screenplay.

Having the whole story in front of me, adapting it to the screen should have been straightforward, but it wasn't. Parts of the book I had never been happy with, and my ideas had changed so radically since I wrote it that I was bound to want other changes. I resolved to throw every filmic idea that had ever trespassed into my mind at the script, and I could shape this raw clay as I went along. My intentions loomed over everything like a great bat—I had included locations from bleak arctic landscapes to arid deserts, and appointed a cast from kings to criminals, super heroes to scullery-maids and back again. In between were cameos by character actors, and CGI never before seen by human eye. Somewhere in there was still the Quest, fighting for survival.

A coherent time frame within the basic three act structure, I kept telling myself, was essential. I also ruthlessly edited anything that was either irrelevant or not funny if it was supposed to be. Preparing detailed visual descriptions focussed my ideas; I was convinced I was making progress. By the time I had finished Version #2 I needed a drink. After a glass or two of the Pinot Noir I reread the script and, deciding all the elements to the story were in place, I fell asleep at my desk. The strange buzzing I heard took me a few seconds to identify. Linda's voice on my phone was all too familiar. She started in before I did.

"My brother's had some problems … I'm in Brighton."

"What's the trouble?"

Linda dismissed my question in her usual way.

"You wouldn't understand …"

"When are you coming back?"

Her icy tone could have sunk the Titanic several times over

"I'm seeing that Greek waiter at the moment."

"What Greek waiter?"

"The one in *Rousso's*."

"He's Spanish, not Greek."

"Well, whatever he is … he's taking me away for the weekend."

I gave up. Was Linda having an affair with a flurry of waiters, or whatever the collective was for serving staff? I realised I didn't care in the least; I was too busy thinking about the script.

* * *

Quatro's, the scene of my debacle with Whitefield, seemed exorcised of his presence when Kenny and I met there on Monday morning. She had taken an early train from London and looked pale, probably from going *Around The World in Eighty Hours* so recently. Kenny hugged me; it was always nice when she did that. The quizzing that followed was less so, as I had a mild hangover.

"The money is in the bank, I checked yesterday."

Kenny nodded perfunctorily.

"Have you got the screenplay?"

"I'll get it over to you today … tomorrow. There's still some fine tuning to be done."

This wasn't good enough, apparently.

"*Jack!*"

"What?"

She looked at me as if I was sub-human.

"Genre … style…? How can I manifest your poetic visions if I don't know anything about them!"

"If you're sarky with me I'll hire another producer."

Kenny stuck out her tongue.

"Go ahead, see if I care. You're a pain in the ass anyway."

We started laughing at exactly the same time; it was a good feeling. Why was it that explaining anything about the movie so difficult for me? I had been in the biz long enough to know that ninety-nine percent of productions were capable of being summed up in a few words, or a handy phrase. I tried, first of all silently to myself. The theme was the

Quest—the hero sets out to get what he wants, by the end he succeeds or doesn't, or he may even get something entirely different. The bit in between was the adventure. Weren't all movies like that? Expect for those tedious exercises by Andy Warhol, of course.

"Get that to me tomorrow morning … or even better tonight … I can't even think about cast or crew until you do. Let's meet here tomorrow afternoon."

We did just that. I had dutifully finished the screenplay and emailed a copy to Kenny. One went to Dolly as well. Kenny and I met as planned, and I was glad to see she was already on the case.

"We can shoot this in six weeks … thirty shooting days."

"As long as we schedule the scenes carefully …"

Out came the file. It was good to see *Paper Sun* on the cover.

"Production Designer … I thought Mick Timble … Casting Director … not sure yet. There's a lot of studio time and sets to build … but if we get started straightaway they'll be ready by the time we've shot the exteriors … say by the end of Week 3."

I was following all this while studying my copy of the screenplay.

"Barstowe first … Cotswolds … Cambridge comes a lot later."

"Quite a bit of Green Screen needed … but the place I'm thinking of using has three studio spaces and over a hundred feet of key screen. It's also five thousand square feet overall, which is just about okay."

"Camera? Phil's retired now I'm sure."

Kenny shook her head.

"Definitely not. He's in his 70s now and I don't think he's very well either … Toby?"

"I'm fine with him … his work on *Billabong* was good."

"Editor? Who do you want?"

"I'd have Jeff, but again, he can't work the hours. *And* I don't know how well he's made the change to digital …"

"He's almost a craftsman from a different era now … I'm not knocking that but …"

Time had caught up with us all. How much had it caught up with me? I gulped quietly. Kenny went through the rest of the crew without much reaction from me. Even the name of the DOP I didn't pay much attention too—that turned out to be a big mistake, though I couldn't have known it at the time.

"I don't know if you've thought about casting yet, but wait for me on that, won't you? Whatever you do don't use Kit Meads. I spent two months last year with that guy, and he is just such a total pain."

I suddenly recalled the strange twilight world actors inhabited—one where I would soon have to venture again myself.

"Be nice to get a few names that sell … and one or two of the old stagers …"

Kenny looked at me in sideways fashion.

"I knew it would end up with me making the suggestions …"

"You're so up to the minute, Kenny, finger on the pulse of showbiz … down with the kids."

"Wotchit! Just bloody wotchit …"

I smiled sweetly. Kenny ignored me and rifled

through her files. I asked if she had hooked up with Boris Cantini.

"He emailed some estimates for US distribution … they look good. Projected gross is a hundred and fifty million dollars."

Pretty fine for a movie with a budget of a third of that figure, I thought, though I could never quite understand how these things got worked out. Even when I saw the breakdown of figures, it didn't make a lot of sense to me, but I went with it anyway. As long as I got my fee as scriptwriter and director I was happy. Together that amounted to $700,000—*a whole chunka change*—as the Americans say. I would also own a fifty-per cent share of the movie's income as soon as it went into profit. What Kenny was now listing all seemed endless.

"Boris details streaming, DVD, Domestic TV, iTunes, Amazon and Netflix, it almost equals the initial profit."

"What about pre-videos, all that teaser stuff …"

"That's all in there as well. I'm gonna get some guys in London to do a website and hit social media."

Kenny and I agreed on a date to start shooting—two weeks after pre-production. A week later, *Strike*—an on-line movie magazine—wanted to film an interview with me. I suggested they do it on set early on Day 1. They liked the idea. The questions would be about as searching as a gaffer asking me what I wanted for lunch from the catering truck, I was sure of that.

19

Being *in front* of a camera was certainly a change. About a thousand things filled my mind at that moment, one of them was the realisation I was about to be interviewed.

STRIKE: Can I ask you a very general question first … as someone about to embark on Day 1 of a feature, how do you see the British Film Industry at the moment?

JACK: It's probably as healthy as it ever will be. It won't change now.

STRIKE: Why do you think that is?

JACK: We haven't got any money in this country!

STRIKE: It's all in Hollywood?

JACK: Yep.

STRIKE: What about independent film right now? Do you see that as flourishing?

JACK: I see some wonderful stuff … and some real crap.

STRIKE: With indie film, when you do see something you like, is it some new, innovative approach that appeals to you?

JACK: Skill, talent, craft … they all go a

long way. Probably more so.

STRIKE: Just those things?

JACK: I like weird stuff too, when I can't tell where it's coming from, same as you get with music sometimes.

STRIKE: And for you, as a director, what's it like making a big movie in England in 2014, I mean from say ten years ago?

JACK: It doesn't seem to change that much, but I'll let you know when we have a wrap! Filming is always a hassle ... working sixteen hour days *and* trying to cope with the weather, *and* all those other things you can never predict. Trying to get it all done is always the challenge.

STRIKE: How about production, has that changed?

JACK: (laughs) You'd better ask Kenny my producer about the problems she has...

STRIKE: Can you tell us? I mean, such as?

JACK: Cost of locations is one. I see the figures Kenny gets from the people who are responsible for setting the fees for these places ... they must be living in another world.

STRIKE: The word 'movie' gets mentioned, and immediately there's dollar signs in their eyes...

JACK: Exactly.

STRIKE: You're known as a director's director...

JACK: I'm never quite sure what that

means…

STRIKE: Someone who actually makes his dream into a reality, perhaps?

JACK: I try.

STRIKE: Now, I have to ask you this … what makes a good director?

JACK: Probably someone who can answer fifty questions at once and make all the answers sound like the mean something. How's that?

STRIKE: You've done very well with ours! Thanks very much.

JACK: My pleasure.

Later I thought a bit more about what I'd said about directing. I'd given a flip answer even though it was true enough. I could have said a lot of things including the analogy of the director being the captain of the ship and bringing his craft (the finished movie) safely in to port. Because making a movie is a communal undertaking, the director relies totally on the people he is working with; he cannot achieve the slightest thing without them. Thus he respects their views and *listens* to them, or should do. Always prepared to change his mind, but ultimately he makes the decisions. There should be a tangible tension on a set too. Right down to the last grip, everyone must be one hundred per-cent involved.

The previous weekend had been spent with Kenny and the crew, arranging and rearranging the first week of shooting. I was so involved I lost all sense of everything else. Relaxing was not on the agenda, unless that was a synonym for being completely knackered. I did consider watching TV when I was at home, but decided I only wanted to see my own movie, jumping out of a giant flat screen, bought, hired and streamed by everyone, all over the world. Age is supposed to bring wisdom, but not in my case, apparently. Everything seemed hunky-dory, and I was the most content I had been for a long, long time. How wrong can you be? At the end of week 1, I suddenly realised it was not a happy ship.

Kenny came up to me after the day's shoot on Friday, obviously wanting to talk. I unlocked my trailer, and we got settled inside.

"Tell me, honestly, how do you think things are going?"

I was stumbling around, and she knew it.

"With getting everything done?"

"No, I don't mean that ... and you know I don't, Jack."

I was treading carefully, wondering if Kenny had seen what was going on in the same way I had.

"Things aren't right on set, are they? Call it my intuition, if you want, but you have to have that in my job."

I hesitated a bit more.

"There are a few things ... everyone getting themselves together on time ... coordinating rehearsals."

"There's something much bigger than that though, isn't there?"

I took a deep breath.

"Yeah ... the big problem is with Hardy."

Kenny looked surprised.

"Hardy ... the DOP? Want to tell me about it?"

"It usually goes like this ... Toby sets up the shot and almost every time Hardy changes it."

Kenny looked the most amazed I'd ever seen her.

"He can't do that!"

"He seems to think he can, and this has kept on happening ... right up until the end of day three."

"That's not good. So how did this pan out then? Did you tell him what he's doing isn't acceptable?"

I sighed, a heartfelt version.

"I tried everything, so did Toby. At first I just laughed it off, then I very quickly realised this was confrontation time ... and there was no way he was going to back down."

Kenny continued to look amazed.

"I can't get my head round this. You'll have to tell me again, slowly."

"Okay. Well, the first day was a bit chaotic anyway ... because of all those problems with sound at the location."

"Right. Right. Those stupid neighbours. I've made sure that doesn't happen again ..."

"Yeah. Thanks. Anyway, I wanted to be up and running on Day Two so I explained in detail to Hardy what I wanted on Monday night. Showed him the story boards and everything."

"And he was okay with that?"

"He was agreeing with me, but you know how people can say 'yes' when they mean 'no.'"

Kenny's eyes went skyward.

"Only too well, I've been putting up with that for

twenty years or more."

"So, after I came back from rehearsal on the morning of Day Two, all ready to go. I knew something was wrong."

"He hadn't given you the look you wanted."

"No, he hadn't."

"And you told him that?"

"At first, I was a bit blown away. I looked at how everything was lit again and checked the monitors. I thought maybe I was having hallucinations or something."

"But you weren't …"

"No. What we had was not what I wanted, but how Hardy thought it ought to be."

"Oh, no!"

I looked at Kenny.

"So what was I supposed to do? You tell me."

"More important, what did you do? I wasn't there remember, and no one has told me about any of this."

"Well, obviously I was pissed off, and I told Hardy that he hadn't lit the set in the way I'd asked for it to be."

"What was his reaction?"

"Just stood there and looked at me as if to say, 'This is the way it's gonna be, I know best. '"

Kenny just stared.

"What! I've never heard of a DOP being like that before."

"I know … really weird. I just got the feeling that *whatever it was* I'd tell him to do he wouldn't do it. It's his way or no way."

Kenny looked genuinely baffled.

"I don't understand. Why is this happening?"

I shrugged.

"It may be something quite simple like the difference between the way they work in America and the way we do it here. The AD was telling me Hardy's worked a lot over there, on some pretty big stuff too."

Kenny was nodding.

"Right. Everyone is answerable to the DOP over there, I remember somebody telling me that too. I've never worked on features in America, you see."

I paused before reloading.

"There's another issue as well …"

"Yeah? What's that?"

"The number of takes."

"How d'you mean?"

"When I cut and want to go on to the next set-up he throws a moody … every time."

"Why?"

"He wants to do another take … the guy is obsessed …"

Kenny considered.

"But an editor likes to build up a scene from a lot of alternative takes, that's pretty basic."

I was a touch exasperated.

"*I know that Kenny*, but not when the actors are getting stale and tired, that doesn't achieve anything. It's counterproductive … the chance of getting some miracle shot on Take 97 is very slim."

"Directors all have different approaches …"

I sat back.

"And in this case Hardy thinks *he's* the director, I'm sure of it."

Kenny shook her head; I could see she was fed up with this already.

"So what happened on Day 4 and 5? You'll have to tell me."

"I took Toby and Steve and Malcolm … in costume … and did some hand held and steadi-cam in the city."

Kenny looked surprised, to say the least.

"You did?"

"Yeah, I told the crew to stand down."

Her eyes were wide.

"Two free days in the first week! They'll love you more than their own mothers."

"Maybe. I'm more worried that they'll work out something's going on …"

"They've probably done that already."

"… *and* Hardy's got a little gang of admirers around him already."

"Really?"

"Girls in the cast … Sara, Liz … Debra … Sharon in make-up too."

I could see Kenny looking more concerned.

"If he's deliberately stirring it, that's bad. As soon as you start getting factions on a set, it's hell for everyone."

I wanted to get back home. Have a shower and probably a glass of wine or two.

"Okay. Well, maybe we'll talk to each other over the weekend."

"I think we'll have to … these things won't just go away …"

Kenny was thinking hard, I knew it. She had a

particular way of looking when she did that.

Sunday night brought the call from Kenny confirming our schedule for Monday and the coming week.

"Now *I've* got problems too …"

"Yeah?"

"Gill and Lisa aren't happy."

"What's the trouble with them?"

"One that will have to be sorted out with … shall we say … diplomacy."

"Really?"

"They don't like close scenes with Brett … his breath smells."

"What! That's basic stuff. Hasn't he read any of those books on movie acting?"

"Obviously not the right ones. He's a big-headed so-and-so, that Brett."

"Yeah, directing him isn't that easy."

There was one of those pauses long enough to make you wonder if the other person is still there.

"You don't think there's any way round the problems you're having with Hardy?"

I must have sounded gloomy.

"Not really. The mistake I made was being nice to him in the first place … trying to reach a compromise … he just saw that as weakness."

"Yeah, some people are like that."

I could tell Kenny was deliberating.

"The problem for me is I can't have a production that's all stop and start. I mean, you've laid the crew off twice already."

"I couldn't think of doing anything else."

"I understand that, but I just don't know where I am. For instance, do I carry on with getting these sets made up or what …"

I was striding about waving my arms about, a sure sign of frustration.

"What do *you* suggest?"

"I'll arrange a meeting with you and Hardy. We have to do that … for my sake at least."

"Yeah, or we'll be wasting even more time …"

"Right, and that will get very tight soon, I know … especially when we get up to Scotland, and those other out of the way places that are on the schedule."

I breathed out.

"It's very difficult to understand what goes on in that guy's head …"

"… or anybody's head."

I rambled on.

"Have you talked to him at all?"

"Yeah, I have. He told me he wants to be back in Hollywood making these billion dollar monster pictures … reckons that's the way ahead."

"So, why did he take this job?"

"Why does any one of us take a job, Jack? Because he needed the money."

This wasn't just professional rivalry with Hardy, there was something else and I knew it.

"Remind me how he got hired again …"

"Hardy came through Boris Cantini. I thought you knew that."

I stopped pacing.

"Boris? But how did Boris know about Hardy? I thought the guy came from Derbyshire or

248

somewhere?"

"He's worked a lot in America. Hardy told me he lives in England, but spends a lot of time in Kentucky I think."

"Kentucky!"

"Does that mean something?"

It might have meant a lot, though I didn't say anything. There was some connection that either didn't make sense at all, or made too much.

"I'll see you tomorrow."

"I'll fix up this meeting, and see how that goes."

I agreed without a lot of enthusiasm. The movie I wanted to make was already turning into the movie I couldn't make, or so it seemed.

In line with vulgar superstition, Monday started off badly and didn't get any better. Another long-held belief, pertinent to the movie world, is that once trouble starts with a production, it goes on happening. When I arrived the first person I saw was Kenny— on her phone, frantically calling people and striding around. When she finished with one call she was obviously ready to make another, but turned to me. She looked more than harassed.

"We can't get that location for Wednesday before 9 a.m. and we have to be out by four. That's completely useless."

"I thought …"

"Yeah, I thought so too, that was the arrangement Eddie made a month ago."

"Can we get more days?"

"More budget …"

"Another location?"

"Transport, catering…that was what was good about that one because it was so central. *And* there's proper loos."

"Keeps the ladies sweet, definitely."

I tried to be helpful.

"Should I have a word with these guys?"

"You can always try."

"Wasn't there a contract with the hours all specified …"

"I left that to Eddie … he made all the arrangements …"

"What does he say about it?"

Kenny shook her head.

"I dunno … obviously wires crossed somewhere."

Decision-making time.

"We'll have to shoot over the weekend, do the other scenes then …"

Kenny looked imploringly at me.

"Jack, you *know* what hassle that causes me."

"Might be the only way …"

She shooed me away.

"Listen, I'll handle all this as best as I can. It's time for you go and see Hardy."

I looked round for the AD as she was talking.

"Alright."

I saw Danny approaching.

"Hi! I have to go off to a meeting, but can you make sure that second unit stuff is ready to go. Fred knows what he's got to do."

I yelled over my shoulder.

"Get to block and rehearse! Say we'll start at … I

dunno … ten?"

I hurried off to a rendezvous I didn't want to make.

20

Kenny had arranged the meeting with Hardy should be in my trailer. He was late, as I knew he would be. When he finally arrived, he was sour and silent. I knew it had to be me who started things off, so I did.

"I'm not happy with your input on the movie."

He was cool.

"You're not, huh?"

"No, and from now on we're going to do it my way and not yours."

Hardy paused to take this in for a moment.

"I have more experience of filming than you do."

"So what? In the end that means nothing. I'm the director. It's *my* movie."

"You're just the guy who wrote the screenplay."

"*And* the director."

"I'm trying to make your film for you …"

"I'd rather you didn't."

He shook his head as if he was a priest dealing with a heretic.

"It's impossible to discuss anything with you. You have totally the wrong attitude."

I couldn't believe I was hearing this stuff. I decided to say my piece and leave at that.

"Look, you've had a negative effect on set, so much so that I've had to stop shooting and stand the crew down twice. We're going to be behind schedule any moment, the producer isn't happy …"

He stared at me, as if to say that none of this could possibly be his doing.

"If you had listened to me you wouldn't have these problems."

This was too much.

"*I did listen* … too much … and I wished I hadn't fucking bothered."

Hardy went very quiet and looked at me with a contempt I had never seen before in anyone. Hatred was in there too and I suddenly thought he might get violent. I waited, watching him carefully, wondering if I shouldn't have had the security guy in here with me, but it was too late now. As it was, Hardy got up and left.

"I'm going to talk to the producer about all this. This is just totally not acceptable. You just do not understand the situation … *or anything that's happening.*"

The voice was verging on hysterical—a man on the edge, spinning round and round, going nowhere.

Unless you hide in a trailer, or find a corner where nobody goes it's virtually impossible to be alone on a film set. I had to get away and the nearest I got to solitude was a corner of the nearest field. It was also where I found Toby, rolling a cigarette.

"Hi."

Toby waved with a circular motion of his hand.

"Okay?"

My expression showed pretty clearly that I wasn't.

"Could be better, a lot better."

"It's strange isn't it … you start a movie and nobody knows where it's going to go."

"I'm just hoping this one gets going before it's too late."

"It's been a bit slow so far …"

I bit the bullet.

"What does the rest of the crew think about it all? If you don't mind telling me about that …"

Toby didn't think for long.

"You'd have to be pretty dumb not to know that something's gone wrong."

I paused to take this in.

"Have you had any hassles … personally?"

Toby didn't seem to want to commit himself.

"From where?"

"Rather … from whom?"

"The DOP?"

I nodded. Toby's expression didn't change much.

"He was a bit in my face at first. Same as he was with you, right? Then he made some comments about the lenses I was using, but I think he realised pretty quickly I knew what I was doing."

I looked at him. Did that mean Toby thought I didn't? I was beginning to wonder if anyone on the set regarded me as anything but an idiot. Toby blew out a stream of smoke.

"I hope we don't get any more trouble, man."

Everything seemed to be getting more and more surreal. When I saw Kenny later she was so casual I wondered if she was acting in a comedy sketch.

"How did your meeting with Hardy go?"

"He's totally insane."

"Isn't everyone in this biz?"

"Maybe, but there are degrees of insanity."

"I wish I knew what they were."

I stared straight ahead of me, at nothing in particular. I was getting impatient with it all.

"Can't we just sack him?"

"Difficult at this stage…

"How d'you mean?

"He's committed himself to a ten week shoot. This is week 3 coming up."

"What's that got to do with it?"

"We're way behind schedule that's why …"

I could see Kenny was looking at all this very differently from me. Hers was exclusively the producer's point of view.

"Okay. I've maybe got a way round it …"

"Which is …"

"I originally wanted to shoot a lot of this like *The French Connection* …"

Kenny was looking doubtful already.

"I want three cameras in there … for the set pieces."

"What will that do?"

"It means we take a third of the time over every scene."

"Jack, it doesn't necessarily work like that …"

"I can set up the master shot, then do the rest like a documentary."

"That'll look terrible …"

"I don't mean for the whole of the shoot ..."

Kenny shrugged.

"Okay. Try it."

I looked round circumspectly.

"And where's our little ray of sunshine right now?"

"Nobody knows ... I think he's off set."

"We ought to plan what we're going to do next week ..."

"I know. I'll call you ..."

I went back to the set and we got half-a-day's shooting in. The way it had been going up until now, I regarded that as a miracle.

I knew there had to be a reason why Kenny didn't call me until late on Sunday. She was quick to tell me why.

"We don't have to sack Hardy ... he called on Friday night and told me he was leaving."

I echoed the words loudly.

"On Friday night?"

Kenny's words came out slowly.

"Yes, Jack, and I've spent most of the weekend finding you another DOP."

"Okay. Thanks, I wasn't ..."

"Yes, you were! I didn't want to talk to you about it until I'd solved the problem myself."

I let the dust settle.

"Okay, thanks."

"I had to drive to fucking Essex this morning to give this new guy the screenplay."

I attempted no jests about Essex girls or anything else; I would have been signing my own death warrant.

"Can we talk about next week ..."

"Frankly, I think we should meet with Toby and the new DOP on Monday and sort everything out."

"Could be good."

"I've had to move the date when we're going to the new location to Wednesday anyway. We might as well finish up totally in Barstowe over the next two days, and then get out to the Cotswolds."

"How long do we need to be there?"

"Originally I planned for eight days in Winchcombe, but we'll have to cut that down … try to get it all finished this week."

"Fair enough. Then we're in the studio, right?"

"If those sets are ready, yeah."

I detected Kenny was in her 'just leave me alone' mood and I did so.

"Okay. I'll see you tomorrow."

Edmund Farrish, the new DOP, was on set promptly on Monday morning. That was a good omen, although I was feeling a tad cynical. I considered that a deaf monkey would be an improvement on Hardy. Edmund looked quite anonymous but, after an initial exchange or two, I was convinced he was competent. I discussed the first set up with him at the same time I was doing the blocking. After the cast had gone off to make-up, I introduced Edmund to the lighting crew. They seemed to respond well enough to his ideas.

Toby, Edmund, and I discussed getting the best out of our Cotswolds location. The honey-coloured stone of the buildings harmonised immaculately with the grassy verges, but I didn't want any hint of some chocolate-box look. I wanted to turn the whole thing on its head, by making the parochial look epic. The stillness of the canals and the whole sublime atmosphere of the village had to be made sharp and full of shadow. Together they worked on getting me the look I wanted and my enthusiasm—rather in abeyance of late—returned.

By Thursday I was tired, and not with the kind of fatigue that comes with satisfaction. The moments of exultation had been there, but the atmosphere on set had suffered badly from the initial disruption and I wondered if we would ever get back on track. While driving the short distance back to the hotel everything went round and round in my head. It was as if everyone, even Kenny, could not escape the malaise of the moment. Outwardly, most of the players appeared calm, but their mood betrayed them constantly.

When I got to the set on Friday morning and saw Kenny waiting for me, I knew there was more trouble brewing. I was right. My intuition had been working overtime all week, probably contributing to my weariness. This time the problem came from where I least expected it. That's often the way with trouble; it sneaks up on you from behind.

"I had a call from America, from a lawyer in New York no less."

"Really? Who was that?"

Kenny fished around in her case.

"Hang on I wrote it all down. They represent Cole Wertheim ..."

"The guy who put up the funding ..."

"Right. These guys are Strand, Bulmer & Flew

LLP and they are private funds lawyers."

"What do they do?"

"Look after their clients' money, in what they call *lawyer trust accounts*."

I shrugged.

"Okay ... so what did these guys want?"

"As far as I can understand it all, some other law firm is employed to monitor these accounts. They wanted to check on where this money went."

"Fair enough, this Wertheim guy put up the funding ... the fifty million dollars ... it's in my production company account in a bank in Louisville. I told you that."

Kenny was equal.

"Maybe you did, it doesn't really matter. These *other lawyers* are sending a *facilitator negotiator* to see you."

"A what?"

"I didn't understand that bit either ... it all got very weird at that point. They wouldn't say what he wanted to talk to you about, or what he does or anything. All I know is he's flying over on the weekend and wants to have a meeting with you on Monday morning."

"But why?"

"Jack, I just told you, *I have no idea*. His name's ... wait a minute ... Marty Cooter. I asked if I could be there in the meeting, that was the least I could do. I thought you might want some support ..."

"Definitely."

"They said that was okay."

"Big of them."

"So we shall see what happens on Monday at 10

a.m."

"I don't suppose these guys think about me trying to make a movie."

Kenny spoke very slowly.

"In the end, all these people worry about is that it's their money you're making the movie with."

My brain started to turn somersaults. I had to get in touch with Boris Cantini and fast. I wanted to know the details about Hardy's appointment as DOP *and* who this Marty Cooter was. The ways of Americans are only ever understood by other Americans. A bit like women who, most of the time, know exactly what each other is thinking, while men haven't a clue.

When I got home I calculated the time difference before calling LA. I reached Boris on his cell phone, as they call them over there.

"Hi, Jack, what's up?

"Quite a lot …"

"Yeah? With this new project, huh?"

"Right …"

"You don't sound too good. Things goin' wrong?

"I certainly hope not, but I think you'll be the man to tell me if they are."

"Maybe. Try me."

"The funding came from a guy over there called Wertheimer."

"Okay. I never heard of him."

"Yesterday his lawyers got in touch with the producer to say they're sending a facilitator negotiator to meet me."

"Oh, yeah? They tell you why?"

"No. That's what worries me."

"What's this guy's name?"

"Marty Cooter."

There was a definite pause.

"Uh, oh … Magic Marty huh? *That guy*."

"Don't keep me in suspense, Boris."

"Wait a second. I have an apology to make."

"You do?"

"There was mail for you at the production company mailbox here in LA … looks like it's from a law company."

"What did it say?"

Boris breathed in.

"Hold it … not so fast. First off, I been outa the state and I only got this mail yesterday. Second, I didn't open it right away, but I got it here …"

I could hear that subtle sound paper makes when it is being torn, then unfolded a few times.

"It's a contract between Butternut and this guy Wertheimer you were just talkin' about."

"So can you give me an idea about what this contract is?"

"I sure can …"

Boris was obviously scanning the document with an experienced eye. I could hear him breathing hard.

"You ain't gonna like this."

"Tell me the worst."

"Basically this Wertheimer guy has total control of the movie."

"What!"

"Everything … artistically, financially … the works. They … meaning him or any of his agents or associates … can make changes in the script, edit anyway they want, or shut you down … all of it."

I was thinking fast, too fast.

"I didn't sign anything like that though. I've never even seen this contract."

"Yeah, that kinda puzzled me too. It has been signed … for and on behalf of Butternut. I saw a signature somewhere here. Lessee … Dolly …"

"Dolly Thorne!"

"That's right."

My head was swirling like a sauna.

"So who is this lady? If you don't mind me askin'."

"She's the one who got the funding from Wertheimer."

"Right … right."

"Do you know her by any chance?"

Boris was thinking almost as fast as I was.

"Wait up! I'm sure she's the one that called me … Miss Thorne … from the South. Way she sounded it coulda been Dolly *Parton* right there."

"You got it. So, what did *she* say to you?"

"She said she represented you *and* Butternut … you had common interests with investment, or something like that. It was a little weird … but I figured no one could make up a story like that … just hittin' on yer name *and* yer production company. I mean yer not *that* well-known over here … in Hollywood, or anything … no offence."

"I'm not offended."

"After I told her I was associated with you and Butternut, she said for me to call up yer producer in England. I had to give her the name of some dude who had to be signed up as the DOP on the picture … that was part of the whole deal."

I was dumb for a moment, then recovered.

"And his name was Hardy Leek, right?"

"Could be … that I really don't remember … it was just a name and a contact number. But I did call yer producer lady. Kenny, right? I remember all that."

"What happened there?"

"I just passed on the details about this DOP guy. I remember she sounded kinda busy, an' was grateful to get the name. One less crew to worry about getting' I guess."

I thought about all this for a long moment.

"Let's talk about that contract. Even though it wasn't signed by me … and has Dolly Thorne's name on it … I'm bound by everything in it, is that right?"

"Sure looks like it."

"It doesn't mean anything that it's *my* production company?"

"Nope, it don't. Everything in this contract just refers to Butternut as the client. The way it's set up, you're just an employee of Wertheimer, that's all there is to it. I'm tellin yuh, buddy … they got you by the balls."

My head was spinning. I thought it might leave my shoulders at any moment.

"And what's this Cooter guy going to do?"

I could hear Boris breathing even harder.

"I gotta say this, they only call him in when they wanna wind down companies, offload staff … all kindsa stuff. He's one helluva operator, I'm tellin' yuh"

I was thinking aloud.

"I've already had one lot of trouble with this Hardy character …"

"You have?"

"Complete freak show".

"I'm so sorry, my friend."

"What I'm worried about is if this Cooter bloke makes me suspend shooting, that'll be the second time on the shoot. I can't make a movie under this kind of pressure."

"People have done."

I knew I couldn't, and this was only the beginning of the nightmare.

Marty Cooter was everything I feared he would be. The moustache that was just too neat and the designer jacket. They all went with the part—the bad guy. God obviously created people like him for some good reason, but one definitely beyond me. On Monday morning at precisely the time appointed he appeared on the set, looking round as if he owned it and everything else in the world. Cooter's smile had an inbuilt flashing device; he turned this on me and Kenny in turn. I didn't respond, so his next ploy was to take Kenny aside.

"Is it okay if we have a word privately?"

That was the moment I knew I was doomed, but determined to go down fighting anyway. Marty and Kenny returned and the three of us gathered in the trailer. He was sitting opposite me, Kenny off to the side. By her look, I guessed she would have preferred to be anywhere but right there at that moment. I wouldn't say I was a violent character, but Cooter looked at me in a way that straightaway made me want to punch him.

"Let me tell you something first, Mr. Strange. My job is to resolve problems, and that's what I'm here to do."

The Boston accent sounded as unreal as everything else about him.

"We've all got to do something in our lives."

He took this calmly enough.

"Can I call you Jack?"

"Why not?"

"Lemme put it like this, Jack, yer particular role in the project means we have to expect charm, charisma, and appeasement. These are the qualities Mr. Wertheimer would automatically expect from anyone directly involved with any of his business projects."

He paused, presumably for some kind of effect. Not getting any response, he continued, rather brusquely I thought.

"Let me ask you this, Jack, do you consider you have these qualities ... or any of them?"

I didn't hesitate.

"Yes."

Cooter looked puzzled.

"I'm sorry. Yes, what?"

"That's the answer to your question."

He turned in Kenny's direction and applied the glossy smile.

"I think we have a communication issue here ..."

Kenny, whose entire existence revolved around working out compromises between different parties, did her best.

"Do we?"

The mask slipped momentarily.

"We sure do!"

Cooter recovered quickly enough, but he obviously felt uncomfortable with the way Kenny and I were looking at him. Rather as a zoologist might peer at an unusual specimen on a slide.

"I'm sorry. Any kind of emotionalism is totally unacceptable in the present situation. Please accept my apologies, I do hope you will."

Kenny was polite, more than I was prepared to be.

"Of course."

"We have a diversity of perspectives, but my door is open on this issue."

He looked pleased with himself. I soon put a stop to that.

"What's that mean?"

Cooter was starting to look ruffled again.

"Communication. I'm so sorry, it is very difficult for me … not being on my own turf. Let's go forward …"

I was getting bored with all this.

"What exactly have you come over here … all the way from New York … to tell me?"

He looked startled.

"There are fundamental issues, Jack!"

I was even.

"Okay, so what are they?"

"We have concerns …"

"Yeah? Problems?"

Cooter came in with the programmed response.

"Please! We don't have *problems*, we have challenges."

"Call 'em what you want."

"Jack, I'm not here to counsel you, just helping you to access your future."

I suddenly felt the not-so-hidden threat.

"You mean by firing me as director? Is that what you're going to do?"

Cooter obviously wasn't used to such bluntness but automatic pilot helped his recovery.

"I realise this may raise issues of job security. But we all have to move on at some time or another."

Hearing this, it was with some difficulty I resisted the desire to hurl myself upon the man. Pummelling his naked flesh until he screamed for mercy was one approach I had in mind.

"Okay. So what have I done that's so wrong?"

Once more, Cooter obviously wasn't used to being pinned down, relying, as he did, on his repertoire of catchphrases. He was obviously flustered.

"Pursuit of excellence has always been a condition of service."

More meaningless crap.

"Some of us are disappointed by your approach to the project."

"Yes?"

"You have failed to display those qualities I detailed before to you."

I eyed him.

"So, wait a minute! How can *you* possibly know that? Have you been sprouting wings and flying over the set with a telescope?"

Cooter started scowling, and Kenny looked uncomfortable.

"Please don't insult me! What I'm putting on the table are undeniable facts!"

I thought quickly. There was only one person who could have retailed any tittle-tattle and that was Hardy. I was angry with that and showed it.

"Bollocks."

Cooter, predictably I suppose, looked shocked.

"Mr. Strange, please! Nobody on my side of the fence has ever used those terms."

I stood up and stood by the trailer door.

"It seems to me that *sitting* on the fence is all you're good for. You want to be careful you don't fall off and bump your stupid, fat head."

This was too much for Cooter; he lost all control and rushed at me, but I was ready for that. I swung open the door and he plunged headlong onto the grass outside. It had been raining during the night and the smart outfit was not improved by his impromptu flight. He lay groaning on the turf, while Kenny could only stare in disbelief.

Kenny called me on Monday night at the hotel in the Cotswolds.

"You didn't take to our Mr. Cooter, then?"

"Slimy little bastard! He wanted me off my own film."

"He didn't actually say that ..."

"Good as."

Kenny sounded long-suffering.

"Jack, how many times do I have to tell you, it's

not you who's funding this movie. There's bound to be pressures from outside. This time it's the lawyers. Any other time it would be the studio."

"Having dealt with both in my time, I'm not sure which is the bigger bunch of bozos."

"Saying that isn't going to help either."

Something about Kenny's attitude was puzzling me; she certainly wasn't telling me everything either. When I arrived on the set on Tuesday morning I knew why she had been holding back. The place was like a ghost town. That early morning hubbub of anticipation that precedes a shoot wasn't there, nothing was.

"What's going on?"

Kenny appeared from behind the trailer, looking more subdued than I had ever seen her.

"The lawyers ... both sets of them ... called me last night, as well as pinging me around a dozen emails. They were all telling me what they want."

"Which is?"

"A change of plan."

"What sort of change?"

Kenny's smile had no warmth in it.

"You should know by now that when an American says that, it means the deal's off."

I froze.

"They've suspended production as of midnight last night. I mailed everybody last night and sent them a text as well. I was up till four doing that."

"Oh, *shit.*"

"A lot of people were pretty freaked ... wondering if they were going to get paid ... I didn't contact you

… I let you get your beauty sleep. Wasn't that nice of me?"

A lot of stuff was going on in my head but I still asked the relevant questions.

"Did these yanks tell you why they're doing this?"

Kenny was patient, very in the circumstances.

"Marty Cooter reported back to them in the States, they then had a meeting and decided you weren't suitable for the project. They definitely wanted me to understand that."

I stared, and carried on doing so for a bit.

"I know they can do all this, I talked to Boris about it."

Kenny nodded in agreement.

"I've dealt with American lawyers before, they're like Rottweilers … they don't give up. The court decisions are totally screwy over there too."

It was my turn for the shrugging routine.

"I can speak to Dolly Thorne."

Kenny looked blank.

"What good will that do?"

"She and Wertheimer have some kind of understanding, they must have. I don't believe he's been consulted about all this."

"You can try … I don't think you'll get anywhere."

Kenny looked around at what was once a film set.

"I've been made legal custodian of the site. Might be a good idea to get your stuff out soonish … that's what I've told everyone else."

If I wanted any more proof I was flying solo from now on that was it. I picked up my bag and went to the trailer. With the script I put some files and the storyboards and a few other things. Kenny was waiting when I came out.

"I've certainly never met anyone in movies like you, Jack."

I couldn't decide whether that was a compliment or not. Like all women, Kenny knew that the lives of men are filled with hopeless relationships and unworldly schemes.

21

Right from the moment she said 'hello' I knew Dolly wasn't going to be any help. Her tone would have registered only just above freezing.

"This is Jack."

She didn't sound any more friendly at being told this.

"Oh, hi. I can't talk too long, my old man's snoopin' around ..."

"Listen, we've had big problems with the movie ... Wertheimer's lawyers have suspended the production."

She sounded genuinely surprised.

"Really? I have no idea why this is happening, if yer askin' me about this. And if you'll excuse me ... I have to go right now ..."

"Wait a minute! Do you know a guy called Hardy Leek?"

"Yes, I do, actually ... I'm very close to him at this time."

It was my turn for the surprises.

"You are?"

"Hardy and I are in love. When he gets back from your country he and I are gonna live together. I'm going to tell my husband I want a divorce ... prolly in the next few days."

I put some words together, something I found hard to do.

"Does your relationship with this guy have anything to do with him working on the picture?"

She was coolly defiant.

"Sure, I told Boris to put him in as the DOP. That was the deal for giving your production company the fifty mill."

My brain didn't seem to want to work.

"You didn't think to tell me, or Boris, what you were doing?"

"What the hell would it matter? Hardy got a job, you got yer picture. Now, I gotta go …"

I wasn't letting her get away that easily.

"I got thrown off the picture as the director because of Hardy … and the lawyers!"

"Well, I'm sorry …"

"*And* you signed that contract without telling me …"

"Maybe I did. So what?"

"Jesus Christ! Is there anything you wouldn't do to get what you fucking want?"

The phone clicked off. My movie was like one of those model aeroplanes I made as a kid. Instead of looping the loop, the wings had fallen off.

Like Boris, Pete was sympathetic, but as hard as the proverbial rock. He had seen it all before—ten times over.

"Movies don't exist without money. Someone has to foot the bill, and these days it's the money people who run the industry … like your guy. The classic movies have been made … way in the past … now the only thing they're good for is to be studied in film school. If they actually are …"

I realised I had been left behind by an industry that was run by people half my age, those who would regard someone like me with a patronising air. How they would regard a genuine disciple of the art like Pete was beyond anyone's imagination.

"Movies have been going downhill since the Sixties, back then it was a genuine art form. Films were a reflection of society. Right now they're totally ephemeral, tawdry and meaningless. A million dollars spent on a pop video! You've got to be kidding."

"Maybe I should never have bothered. …"

"C'mon, Jack, think about it. *La Mer* got made, *Billabong* got made! They won prizes and made money. You had *some* creative control."

Pete was right, I ought to congratulate myself that once or twice it went right, rather than wallowing in regrets. What I didn't know, and how could I, was that Pete was dying. It was the last time I would hear his voice. Though I never met the man who became my mentor and more, I could always imagine the place where he lived. The bound copies of *Sight and Sound*, the racks of DVDs, and videos, the 8mm movies and a projector. Pete's whole life had been films, he had lived them, nearly as much as I did. The only difference was he had never set foot on a set.

Later, I was to learn that Phil had gone too. All had changed, my dreams and his died at the same time. Did it matter that I would never make another movie? In 2014 Jack Strange quit the movie biz. Did the world stop turning on its axis? I don't think so.

It did take long before I found out that the funds in my account had been frozen by court order in the US. When I contacted Widear and Butterball, the lawyers representing Wertheimer, I actually got to speak to Prescott Widear. He passed me over to Horatio Butterball. The man was as friendly as a cobra on a hot day.

"On behalf of our client, we shall cite the Sarbanes-Oxley Act of 2002."

"What's that?"

"I shall *try* and explain it to you, Mr. Strange. We have overwhelming evidence that insufficient disclosures were made at the time of implementing the contract thus making it null and void. Any claim for compensation you may make with regard to your involvement on this project is thus unsupportable."

"Are you going to do that to everyone who worked on the movie? Rip off, not only me, but all the cast and crew at the same time?"

"Yer remarks are offensive, Mr. Strange, yer crossing the line."

The phone clicked off, but the fight was only just beginning. The movie was never completed; I had no reason to suppose it would be. Wertheimer's company owned everything that had been shot. What use was it to anyone? I never did find out what happened to it; maybe the hard-drive is still languishing on a shelf somewhere. The real reason the funding was pulled came down to Wertheimer's lawyers attempting to save some ailing company he owned, one of many. He did appear to listen to his conscience, or his lawyers, sometime after, and paid everyone involved. My own lawyers kept beavering away and, although I had to wait nearly two years, eventually I got a $1m pay off.

After all this, some might have said I became an eccentric. I let the house become a shambles of books and papers. The garden was a miniature jungle—a haven for any creatures who took up residence there. To save myself joining them I decided a change was needed. I sold the Richardson Gardens and went to live among the Redwoods in Northern California. Missing civilisation, or such as passes for that abstract noun in America, I moved to Wallingford, a district of Seattle. I took up writing poetry and painting watercolours. Sometimes at night I would recall Clinton and hear the music of its church bells.

ABOUT THE AUTHOR

Gordon Strong was born near Glastonbury, Somerset, and currently lives in the West of England. He is an author, speaker and musician with an international literary following. His studies of myth, legend and the esoteric embrace such diverse subjects as Merlin, The Arthuriad, The Holy Grail, Neolithic monuments, Tarot, Magic and the Qabalah.

Now solely involved in writing fiction, his fantasy novels create a hilarious, yet often profound world, one displaying his endless, cosmic imagination. Of his varied and prolific writing career he states:

"I observe, reflect and experiment—from the sum of this and more my writing appears."